BEYOND THE SHADOW OF SAWTOOTH RIDGE

Joni's Story

Beyond the Shadow of Sawtooth Ridge
Copyright © 2022 by Bernie McAuley. All rights reserved.

Published in the United States of America

ISBN Paperback: 978-1-958030-37-0
ISBN eBook: 978-1-958030-38-7

All rights reserved. No part of this publication may be reproduced, stored in a retrieval system or transmitted in any way by any means, electronic, mechanical, photocopy, recording or otherwise without the prior permission of the author except as provided by USA copyright law.

The opinions expressed by the author are not necessarily those of ReadersMagnet, LLC.

ReadersMagnet, LLC
10620 Treena Street, Suite 230 | San Diego, California, 92131 USA
1.619. 354. 2643 | www.readersmagnet.com

Book design copyright © 2022 by ReadersMagnet, LLC. All rights reserved.
Cover design by Rachel Firkins
Interior design by Daniel Lopez

BEYOND THE SHADOW OF SAWTOOTH RIDGE

Joni's Story

BERNIE MCAULEY

ReadersMagnet, LLC

I would like to express my special thanks of gradtitude to these people my good friend for designing and painting the cover Rachel Firkins. Steve Lawerence for doing the editing of this book and entering his comments. Rick Cole one of the original Navy Seabees Engineers based on Diego Garcia. His knowledge of the island. Loaning me his knowledge. And to my lovely Wife Linda McAuley for the support.

TABLE OF CONTENTS

Prologue	The Cottonwood Stump	ix
Chapter 1	Naval Academy	1
Chapter 2	Naval Flight Training	3
Chapter 3	Flight School	6
Chapter 4	Texas Flight School	10
Chapter 5	Thanksgiving with a Texas Family	12
Chapter 6	First Cross-Country Flight	18
Chapter 7	Christmas At Home	21
Chapter 8	Navy New Year's Eve Ball	26
Chapter 9	Phase Two Flight Training	30
Chapter 10	Carrier Landing	33
Chapter 11	Next Assignment	40
Chapter 12	Mother and Daughter Adventure	43
Chapter 13	Home Between Assignments	56
Chapter 14	Whidbey Island Naval Air Station	64
Chapter 15	My Father's Last Mission.	67
Chapter 16	Christmas Eve	72

Chapter 17	A New Year	84
Chapter 18	Spring Time In Montana	92
Chapter 19	Listening to Nature	101
Chapter 20	Rumors of War	107
Chapter 21	War	109
Chapter 22	Desert Storm Assignment	117
Chapter 23	Monitoring Drug Movement	126
Chapter 24	Returning to Whidbey	139
Chapter 25	Mark's Graduation	152
Chapter 26	Return to Work	159
Chapter 27	It's a Party	166
Chapter 28	Life after the Party	171
Chapter 29	Home for Fall Ranch Duties	180
Chapter 30	New Orders	191
Chapter 31	Operation Southern Watch	198
Chapter 32	The Squadron Returns	205
Summary		217

This story is fictional and work of the authors imagination. The names of the characters are fictional and ranch is also fictional. Sawtooth Ridge is an actual area that sits on the Eastern Front of the Rockies in Montana.

Follow the dreams of Joni as she travels in her father's footsteps as a Naval fighter pilot. She enters a man's world to become one of the best in her class among men. However, being a woman TOPGUN pilot brings challenges that enfold her personal and professional life. Along her path, she learns about her father and the respect he has earned from his time as a POW and top Naval and airline pilot. She also finds the love of her life sitting next to her on a return holiday trip back home which leads her to examine her parents' own marriage. Her birth mother, who passed away before her father returned from Vietnam, seemed to be with her on this path.

Beyond The Shadows of Sawtooth Ridge

Joni Becker Story

PROLOGUE

The Cottonwood Stump

My father always told me if I needed to do some thinking on my own, the place to do it was sitting on the large cottonwood stump (El Tocon) and listening to nature as the creek winds its way down from the Rockies. It was June, and I was home on leave after graduating from the Naval Academy just before starting flight school in Pensacola, Florida. After returning from Vietnam as a prisoner of war, my father had spent many days here trying to clear his mind and soul.

When my mother passed away, I was just a second grader, and my father was a POW in Vietnam. He was released a few months later. My brother and I hardly knew him because he missed so much of our childhood. He had decided just before leaving the hospital to purchase his family's ranch. Our family had returned home to Minneapolis where he tried without a mother and a wife to put the family back together. It just wasn't working for any of us.

He left after a few weeks to create a new home for our small family located on the eastern slopes of the Rockies in The Shadows of Sawtooth Ridge. Here is where we made our home after he returned to flying for an airline. Our mother's grandparents joined us and helped everyone to get settled. His love for this part of Heaven, as he called it, became our dream.

D.D., as everyone called her, entered our lives that same summer. Our father, Mark, and I flew out from Minneapolis for the weekend because dad wanted to show us our new home. It would be an adventure for our entire family since he had spent a large part of the summer training for the airline. The three of us fitting into a two-seat airplane was exciting. Watching him expertly flying for the first time not only was exciting, but it also instilled a dream to fly just like him.

After landing on the small grass strip, we walked to the house. Our father believed contractors usually take weekends off, but entering the house, we heard a sound from one of the bedrooms of glass breaking, a hard knock on the floor, and a cluster of four letter words. I ran to the commotion before he could stop me. Sitting on the floor with a ladder beside her was a lady in distress and very upset after seeing me enter the room. We learned her name was Dakota, or D.D. for short. She and our father had known each other since high school, but as she put it, "Your dad was always too busy to pay attention to a barrel racer." D.D. became good friends with all of us, including our grandparents; as time went on, she eventually became our stepmother.

Both of them became rock-solid stable in our lives. Dad taught us to do well in school, and to fly both the little two-seat airplane and then the dual engine one. Mark and I could fly and solo when it came to our 16th birthdays and I finally learned how to fly a jet by the time I was 20.

D.D. was always there, teaching me to write, cook, and of course, ride the barrels. When I had my heart broken for the first time, she was there for me with a shoulder to cry on. She and our father were both there with us throughout our lives. They cheered us on as we played basketball, baseball, football, and soccer and at high school rodeos. They supported us at teacher conferences through graduating high school and college. This is my story of being a woman and becoming a Naval Fighter Pilot.

1

NAVAL ACADEMY

When I made an announcement one evening at dinner in my senior year of high school that I wanted to attend the Naval Academy, both of them seemed somewhat surprised. Our father had continued to fly for the Naval Reserve out in Washington State once a month besides flying for an airline every six weeks or so. Next to horses and cattle, flying was his second love. It took me a couple of weeks to prepare the application and a personal letter. He had his letter of recommendation to the Naval Academy ready to accompany mine, signed as a Captain (USN). Although his rank and history of being a POW would automatically confirm an appointment, he also added that he wanted his daughter accepted on her own record and not his. Our parents always encouraged us to create our pathway instead of depending on theirs.

Somehow even with both Mark and me in college our parents always seemed to make special days. When I graduated, our father showed up in uniform for the first time in four years. He had been asked to say a few words at the ceremony and hand out the diplomas. My friends were surprised when they learned that he was my father—standing back to salute him after he presented me the diploma. For the first time in my life, I finally figured out that I had a real hero for a father, not only in my eyes, but in everybody else's as well.

He had spent four years as a POW. Then returning home just after my mother, Eve, passed away, he put together the family, became a successful rancher, took on PTSD, continue flying for the reserve, and finally kept alive his passion to again work for an airline. He never took credit for the trail he blazed. His family came first, and he gave his family credit for believing in him. It took many years before I realized why my mother married him, and why D.D. had been in love with him since high school.

2

NAVAL FLIGHT TRAINING

A short time later, my family crammed my duffle bag into the small baggage compartment of the family's Cessna 310. Dad had found this aircraft sitting at an airport in Washington State. He and D.D. always wanted a larger aircraft so the whole family could go along. That was six years ago, and before it came home, he had to make the runway longer and pave it. Soon it became another summer project while the haying, harvesting, and branding were taking place.

It was September when we flew to Washington State to bring the newest member of the family back. I had just turned 16 and had my license to fly a single-engine aircraft. Dad had let me be the co-pilot and fly part of the way home. A year later, both Mark and I qualified to operate it by ourselves. In comparison, while most of our friends were earning their drivers' licenses we were acquiring our flying certificates.

This morning, our parents let me assume the left seat while Mark took the right seat. In his usual unromantic way, our father informed us that he and D.D. were taking the rear seats so they could make out on their way to Great Falls. The sun was high in the sky as we raced down the runway and lifted into the morning air. We made a left turn after take-off and left the ranch behind.

It would be Christmas before I'd return to this home that I had known for so many years—leaving today for Pensacola, Florida, where I would be spending the next six weeks of intensive training. It was the same flight school my father had attended after he graduated from college.

The only difference was that he and D.D. had graduated from a state university. I had graduated from the Naval Academy. Outside of a few dates along the way, my social life was almost nil ever since I wanted to be a naval pilot, and being a female did not help. There were very few of us in the Academy and the flight program, so the few created our own trail. Being on the Naval Academy swim team and the girls' basketball team was a plus in this program. Thanks to my father, I also had my commercial pilot's license before leaving for the Academy. As a result, I felt I had a jump on many others for flight school, including the men.

Mark called the tower for permission to land and let them know we would be taxing over to the aviation terminal and parking temporarily. "Congratulations to you, young lady. It looks like your parents are in the back seat making out today with the kids flying."

A smile of embarrassment appeared on our faces as Mark answered back, "Yes, they are, and someday us so-called kids are going to meet you since you know our parents so well."

When Mark released the button on the mike, we could hear laughter in the background as I was preparing to land the aircraft. Finally, we taxied up to the aviation terminal and parked. Both Mark and I got out and chocked the plane. Our father and D.D. exited with my duffle bag. He looked comical, carrying it over his shoulder to the aviation terminal's car, and then taking us over to the main terminal.

As we exited the car at the main terminal, he proceeded to carry the duffle bag to the ticket counter. All of the employees knew our father and had watched as we had grown into adults; one had even officiated at some of our basketball games. Whenever I checked in, one of them usually said to me, "You look so much like your mother." My father would look at me with a proud smile.

Leaving my family behind was always challenging, and today wasn't going to be much different. My step-mother once told me when they were alone that my father always had a tear in his eye when one of us left. Today wasn't going to be any different, she surmised. The aircraft was now a DC-10 with lots of room in it. Since I was still flying as an employee dependent, I could sit in first class if it was open. The aircraft departed the gate, and I could see my parents and brother Mark standing in the terminal windows waving to me. This flight would end in Chicago, where I would make the subsequent transfer to Florida.

3

FLIGHT SCHOOL FLORIDA

Flight school was an intensive 6-week course with engineering, aerodynamics, air navigation, aviation physiology, water survival, and learning the Morse code. My father informed me that the Morse code had become a means of communication while in prison.

My preferred field was eventually training as a strike pilot and remaining in Florida. However, I would not know if I could prepare for my chosen field until the end of six weeks. It depended on so many different circumstances, including my preferences, my standing in class, and service needs. In the upper ten percent of my class, graduating from the Naval Academy, and already holding my pilot's licenses with all of their endorsements, most of my classmates and instructors felt I had a chance to fulfill my dreams. The one factor against me was being female, supposedly in a man's world, even though many women were more qualified than many men.

The third week, I flew the T-34 with an instructor after countless sessions in the flight simulator. It seemed quite a bit smaller than the twin-engine family Cessna I usually flew, but more fun. The instructor on the first session just requested me to do some basic flight procedures: stalls, crosswind landings, and engine out systems requiring me to find the perfect landing area. I guided the aircraft more than five miles before he finally brought the engine back online.

When I looked at him out of the corner of my eye, there was sweat rolling down his face. My perfect landing area was a freeway, and I managed to find room between a couple of semis. Somewhere down deep, this guy needed a lesson about this girl. Once he returned the engine online, I brought the aircraft almost straight up vertically and did a roll as I leveled off. "Mister, pardon my language, but who in the hell taught you to fly?"

"My father! He was an A-7 Corsair ll pilot in Vietnam off the aircraft carrier Constellation."

Now it was his turn as he took over the controls and started to show me some fancy maneuvers. Finally, he handed over the controls, and I proceeded to copy him. It was like two kids with a new toy trying to outdo each other.

It was the fourth week when I reported for a psychological interview, which made me somewhat nervous. Instead of one psychologist, there were three. The one in the center, whom I felt outranked the other two, asked the first question. "How is your father doing these days?"

Surprised, I replied, "He is doing all right, still flying for the Naval Reserve, and flying as a captain on the 'whale'." He smiled and informed me that we had met earlier.

"You were a little girl when we last met at the Veteran's Hospital in Washington; your father had PTSD when I first met you. Four years as a prisoner of war will do that to you, mister."

"Yes, sir," I replied.

"Does he ever get to the point where he is short-tempered?" the psychologist asked me.

"He does once in a while, but he has a special cottonwood stump down by the creek where he spends time meditating."

As I was beginning to wonder if this conversation was for me or about my father, the officer just smiled and said, "Good Man." Then they all started grilling me on everything from the last several years in the academy plus every part of my personal life, just like I was starting as a freshman again.

Two hours later, it was over, and the officers dismissed me. The naval officer in the center that knew my father finished off as I was leaving the room, "Tell your parents that Phil says hi. I've enjoyed my conversations with both of them over the years. They are very special people."

"Yes Sir," I replied. Finally, it was time to relax as I looked for a place away from the crowd for a bit of peace. The last two hours seemed like the most prolonged two hours of my lifetime.

Ever since my mother passed away, I would lay in bed at night just crying silently, reaching out to my mother in Heaven, not knowing if she was listening or not. One evening D.D. walked in and saw the tears and the redness in my eyes. I did not want her to see the tears, fearing what she might say. D.D. sat on my bed and asked me why the red eyes. I slowly explained to her that I was trying to talk with my mother.

"There is nothing wrong with that. You know both of my parents are in Heaven, and I am a big girl, and I do the same as you. They sometimes answer back but mostly listen. The more you talk, the better you feel." She then reached over and held me in a tight hug and gave me a kiss.

The following two weeks just before graduation went by very slowly. Both Liz, my classmate from Annapolis, and I learned we were going to flight school in Texas. For the first time, neither of my parents were going to be in Pensacola for a graduation. Everyone felt this was the first phase of something bigger to come.

4

TEXAS FLIGHT SCHOOL

I called home the evening before leaving Pensacola. Just like the last 17-21 years, my parents offered encouragement and listened as I talked. My brother, Mark, was accepted for veterinary medicine school in Pullman, Washington after finishing up his senior year at college. Our grandmother was there and joined in the conversation. Grandma mentioned that our mother would be proud of both of us kids and was most likely looking down from Heaven with a smile.

Liz and I made our way to Kingsville, Texas, for Jet-Strike training in the T-2 Buckeye. My grandmother answered the phone this time. Dad and D.D. were out in the field harvesting wheat. It felt strange that I was not there helping out with the ranch's summer duties. When we ended our conversation, I informed her that when Liz and I found an apartment I would call back with the new information.

I was surprised that my father answered the phone the following evening. He must have felt it was time to fill me in on the next chapter of my life. His first question was, "Remember all the things your flight instructors and I taught you about flying?"

"Yes," I slowly replied.

"Well Joni, forget it and everything else we taught you. You will now learn a whole new way of flying, so don't get them mixed up—try to keep them separate. All of your qualifications, licenses, and endorsements are worthless now. Whatever you do, understand I've been there and done it."

My father's advice hit home the next day when the instructors told all of us the same thing as we began our training. It would be 13 months of intensive training on the hot and dry Texas prairies with only a couple of weeks off for Christmas. It would be months before I even had a chance to fly the T-2 Buckeye.

There were several weeks of ground training and over 90 hours in the aircraft simulators before climbing into the real deal. Altogether, there would be 16 flight stages to the entire program. The actual flying time would be more than 100 hours. In the first few weeks, there was intensive ground classroom instruction, simulator training again for a different aircraft, systems training, armament training, and daily physical training. Our days became weeks, and the weeks became months.

5

THANKSGIVING WITH A TEXAS FAMILY

Thanksgiving became a special time for both Liz and me, with a four-day weekend. Both of us had an invitation for dinner with a ranching family near Bishop, Texas. The family requested us in particular. Neither one of us knew anyone that lived in Texas.

Small compared to many Texas ranches I had read about before coming to Texas, we drove up the driveway through the yard to the house, wondering what was in store for us. The family was waiting for us at the yard gate, including two sharp-looking guys and one girl. Liz gave me that funny, bold look and informed me that she had dibs on the guy on the right. We laughed as we exited the car and walked towards the gate. Both of us wore civilian clothes instead of our Class A uniforms. The older man whose name was Ben introduced us to the members of his family. We then moved inside to a large living room with a rock fireplace overlooking the Texas prairie. Everyone was seated except Laura, his wife, and Jill, the sister, who disappeared into the kitchen.

The boys finally broke the ice between everyone in the room. We all started to get acquainted and learned about each other's backgrounds.

Liz was the first to answer their inquiries, a bit nervously, but she answered all their questions. Both her parents were in the military and had met in the service. She had traveled all over the world. The State Department now employed her father, and both parents lived in Arlington, Virginia. Although her parents' background and her grade point were both above average, she had a challenging time getting into Annapolis. When she finally did make the grade and set her goals on being a pilot, no one was going to stop her. I was proud of her since she only received her private pilot licenses while in the Academy.

The oldest boy, John, had just graduated college and was drafted by a professional baseball team before graduation. He was with a couple of their farm teams last baseball season, and would be back for next spring training. Robert, his younger brother, who I thought was sharp-looking, was a college senior this year and had applied to a few veterinary schools. One of them was in Pullman, Washington, where Mark was planning on attending.

I spoke up, saying, "My brother had been accepted there the last time I'd talked to my parents."

Their father then entered the conversation, asking me, "Where are you from, young lady?"

"Montana, sir. We have a ranch on the Eastern Front of the Rockies."

His face lit up, and a smile appeared. "Your father's name is Larry Becker and your mother's is Dakota, aren't they?"

Looking questioningly at him I replied, "Yes, how did you know?"

His wife, hearing the conversation, came out of the kitchen smiling and looked at me like I was a long lost daughter. Her husband started to explain. "Well, your dad and I competed against each other in college rodeo many years ago. I remember he was an excellent calf roper, and he took grand at the National Intercollegiate Rodeo in Denver in his senior year. Dakota and Laura are good friends who trade Christmas cards and sometimes call each other.

Laura smiled and said, "We were so happy that those two finally got married after so many years. Dakota has been in love with your father since they were in high school. After spending four years together on the team, she was upset that he never even asked her for a date. Dakota followed your father pretty closely even after he married someone else. When she met your mother, Eve, I felt she gave up hope of ever getting together with him. I understood that your mother was not only beautiful, but outgoing and smart. Dakota and her sister liked her. She called me just as soon as the military announced that your father was missing in action. We both cried because he was such a great guy. Dakota and I talked to each other over the phone a few weeks back. That's when we found out her stepdaughter was training here. We specifically requested you and Liz when we called the base to offer our home for Thanksgiving dinner."

I could not believe that tonight I was hearing the other side of my stepmother's love story with my father. They hadn't even dated until dad took her out to dinner one evening in Great Falls. They honeymooned in Maui. It seemed their entire life was Mark and me. Once in a while, they would get on their horses and go off for a ride. D.D.'s only comment about their earlier life was that, "Your dad wasn't interested in a 'barrel racer'."

Their daughter, Jill, started asking us all sorts of questions about our professions. Finally, we both clued her in that we were Annapolis graduates and friends who wanted to be pilots. My father was a pilot, and Liz's father was in the military. We let Jill know it was hard being in a so-called male's world. Her brothers made funny faces.

Dinner was delicious and our first home-cooked meal in months. Before we accepted their invitation, we had the choice to stay overnight with them. Since knowing dinner might be late in the afternoon and we might be driving back to base on a dark, moonless night in a strange area, we accepted both dinner and the overnight stay, with breakfast in the morning.

The boys escorted us out to the barn after dinner, with their sister in tow at their mother's urging. It was a beautiful barn with all the trimmings of an indoor arena used for shows or working cattle. Robert took a couple of horses out, and he handed me the lead rope of one of them. "Let us see how good of a rider you are." I looked at Jill and asked if I could use her saddle. Jill made her way to the tack room and brought her saddle to me. I took the saddle and saddled the horse. All of this time, John, with Liz tagging along, was bringing some cattle into the arena. Robert was the first into the arena upon his horse.

"Wondering if you have ever done cutting before," he said with a questioning face.

"Yes," I replied to under my breath as I thanked D.D. for having the patience to work with both Mark and me. He gave me a nod to go ahead and be the first to cut a steer out. Like D.D. had shown me, I entered the herd and picked out one I felt would give me a high grade. I was pretty surprised that my horse quickly picked up on the steer. Then my competitive mood kicked in, and I decided to show off and wrapped the reins around the saddle horn. The horse followed my direction and made me look better than I ever thought possible.

Robert looked at me and smiled saying, "My turn," as he entered the herd and cut his steer out and masterly worked him like he had done it all of his life. Although only early evening, the darkness had closed in on the Texas prairies. Together we pushed the herd back outside, unsaddled our horses, and brushed them down.

Liz walked around the front of the horse while I was taking the saddle off. "You know your stuff. Did your father really do rodeo?"

"Yes, I replied. Both of my parents did high school, college, and pro. However, my father felt the Navy provided him a better opportunity than rodeo did." "I guess he was right, but I always wondered if he was sorry he had made that decision while sitting in prison as a POW for four years."

I shook my head, silently wondering how life would have been if he had finished his tour of duty, had returned home, and my mother had lived. But instead, it had been a Thanksgiving like no other—I learned more about Dad's and D.D.'s relationship than I had known in the 15 years our family had been together.

The family spent the rest of the evening entertaining us with their family music. Finally, Liz and I retired when it just became too late. The boys walked us to our respective bedrooms. Robert asked me for my address and wondered if we could get together some free weekend. I gave him my address and informed him that I was very busy with training, but I would answer his letters if he wrote. Liz did the same with John. The drive back to the base the following day was full of conversation.

It was an enjoyable Thanksgiving for sure. I had to call home, and both parents answered the phones, and grandma joined in the conversation. Unfortunately, it was snowing there, and it looked like it would be more snow for the weekend. My father had another Orient trip in the middle of the week. Mark would be returning to school on Monday, providing the weather improved.

They asked about my Thanksgiving, and of course I described to them that it was a family that owned a quarter horse ranch. I even told them about this young man who thought I was just another girl that he had to teach how to ride a horse. I finally said to them that they knew both of you. Neither one of them seemed surprised for some odd reason. The last piece that I passed along to them was about my first cross-country flight on Monday. Both of them wished me luck and to enjoy the adventure of new airports.

6

FIRST CROSS-COUNTRY FLIGHT

Monday morning after Thanksgiving, I had my first solo cross country flight with the T-2 Buckeye. The Professional Flight Instructor (PFI) seemed to be satisfied with my flying. Up until now, I had been practicing night familiarization flights, formation, and land-based carrier flights. At 0700 the instructor handed me the flight plan. Instead of just taking it and assuming every item was a go, I returned to the flight operations office to check the flight plan one more time. Finding out that I had an extensive weather system along the way, I made sure the flight's fuel load was sufficient to carry me through the entire flight. Exiting the office, the instructor was waiting for me. "Mister, don't you trust your training officer?"

"No, sir."

He smiled at me with a smirk and replied, "Good judgment, mister, dismissed."

It was the usual pre-check when one of the ground personnel opened the cockpit up to enter. "Don't be nervous, mister. Everyone goes through this."

"Thank you, seaman," I replied as the canopy was closing.

My family's Cessna cruised at 225 MPH. This T-2 Buckeye cruised at over 500 MPH. The Cessna's ceiling was about a max of 19000 feet; the T-2 was 45000 feet. I was supposed to be alone on this one. The instructor was to sit and make sure the flight was uneventful. He sat up and behind me.

It looked like he was sound asleep leaning up against the canopy less than halfway into the flight. I made the two required touch and goes at different bases before returning to our base. I tried waking him several times but to no avail. Shortly before landing at our home base, I decided to try one more maneuver doing a couple of barrel rows. He finally awakened, trying to rub his eyes. I tried to keep composed when I asked him, "A little too much partying over the weekend, sir?"

The PFI just groaned and said, "Nice flight, mister."

Three days later, I received a written note from the lead PFI. "Mister, I need to see you in my office at 0800 tomorrow morning."

It was a sleepless night, wondering what I had done wrong. I was standing at attention at his secretary's desk at 0755. He came through the same door as I had a few minutes earlier. "Please come into my office, mister." Reluctantly, I followed him into the office and stood attention before his desk. "Relax, mister. This discussion isn't about you."

Looking at me, searching for the right words to express himself, he finally said, "I have been listening to the flight recorder of your cross-country flight 2 days ago. Just about the entire flight, I heard someone snoring, and I presumed it was your trainer. You tried communicating with him several times but could not. So you did a barrel row to see if you could bring him to. He finally came to just before returning to your home base. You handled the entire situation and flight quite well, but you did not report the incident to his commanding officer."

"Sir, I apologize for that, but I thought it a bit out of line for a junior officer and trainee to do that."

He looked at her straight in the eye. "Mister, you are an excellent pilot. You completed the cross-country solo without an instructor on board. You managed to do it on your first attempt with very little trouble. Who taught you to fly, mister?"

"My father did, sir."

"Does your father fly also?"

"Yes, sir, he trained in the same aircraft that I am training in right now."

He looked at my name for an extended period and then looked at me as he finally remembered who my father was. "You can tell your father that he did a damn good job. Dismissed, mister."

7

CHRISTMAS AT HOME

Christmas leave finally came, and both Liz and I could not wait to leave the base and drive to the nearest airport. I had eventually purchased a car, so it was my turn. My father had made the reservation, and it was through Seattle. So from the time he mentioned to me about the reservation, I wondered, "Why Seattle?" I finally figured it out after I made the transfer to Seattle. The only flight to Montana from the nearest airport did not leave until the following day, which meant overnight sleeping in an airport. Though Seattle, it meant one more transfer but arriving in Montana at a reasonable time.

Deplaning in Seattle, my father was standing there in a naval aviator flight suit instead of a company pilot uniform. I was surprised to see him in uniform. He explained that he had been up to Whidbey (Whidbey Island Naval Air Station) doing his monthly duty just after returning from his trip. He grabbed my handbag just like a gentleman should and carried it to the next gate with his airline flight bags tagging along behind. The fact was, both of us in uniform made me proud to walk alongside him.

People looked at us, and a few even thanked us for our service. I had no idea which one of us was more proud of the other. We finally made it to the gate, where two boarding passes for first-class seats were waiting. One of the older agents looked at me and remarked. "You look just like your mother. She was a beauty and well liked by all of us." I just blushed. It seemed like all the company employees always compared my looks to my mother's.

Even though rain was continuously falling outside the concourse windows, my Christmas leave was starting just as I had envisioned for the past six months. D.D., Mark, and our grandmother were waiting for us when we arrived in Great Falls. The drive home through a raging snowstorm was nothing unusual for Montana this time of year.

Upon arriving home, I had found that D.D. had changed my bedroom somewhat, adding photos from Annapolis and other images I had sent home over the years. A queen size bed had replaced my smaller single bed. D.D. followed me into the room to see my reaction. It was beautiful! I gave her a big hug. "I love it!"

Then she asked me, "How did you like the family you spent Thanksgiving with?"

"They were nice," I replied.

She smiled just a little bit. "Yes, Laura and I have been friends since college. We could not wait until we met the following year at the Intercollegiate Rodeo. Since then, it was Christmas cards and an occasional telephone call that would last for hours. According to Laura, Robert liked you, and John fell in love with Liz."

I replied, "Robert and I had been exchanging letters and telephone calls, but right now, we both have more important items on each of our lists. He has his heart set on veterinary school, and I hope he makes it happen." D.D. just smiled and left the room to start dinner while the men were outside doing the chores. I unpacked my gear and joined D.D. and our grandmother in the kitchen.

Since almost everyone in the family was now an adult, Christmas was slightly different each year as we all became older. D.D. was still into painting and writing for major newspapers. She had a couple of books on various Best Seller Lists. The painting this year was of all of us with Dad and me in our respective uniforms. My father's family started returning for the holidays to the ranch during Christmas like they used to when his grandparents were alive. So once again we always had a full house.

This Christmas the weather was no different than in the past. Our grandfather passed away almost a year ago. He and Grandma seemed to have an exceptional marriage even though our mother, Eve, was their only child. He was a Korean War Vet, and like my dad had PTSD. They pretty much had adopted D.D. even before dad married her. Both my father and D.D. always put the grandparents first whenever the time came. Dad made sure Grandma was at my graduation from the Naval Academy, and I am sure she would be there for Mark's graduation next spring from the university.

Christmas Eve dinner was exceptional with the opening of only one present each. My father sat down at the piano and played several Christmas songs and then some just plain relaxing music. Christmas breakfast and dinner were major events in our home. Grandma made her favorite pies, and on Christmas Day the men cooked the turkey and the ham.

Christmas night, after everyone had gone, D.D. and I were sitting in front of the fire with a glass of wine just discussing life in general, and maybe my own life as it was then. My stepmother knew I was returning to Texas early since Liz wanted to attend a New Year's Eve dance ball.

Neither one of us had a date, but plenty of men had asked. We felt dating someone from our pilot group was out of the question. There was an imagery line between us, and both of us wanted to keep it that way until after receiving our wings. Some of the male personnel were bringing their civilian girlfriends or their wives to the dance.

Out of nowhere, my mother asked, "What about Robert and John as your dates?"

"Come on, mother, they are cowboys and ranch boys. Both of them most likely have never even worn a real suit in their lives. Besides, they would be out of their comfort zones."

"You don't think your dad cleans up real well, just because you've always seen him in his jeans around here. Besides that, he still has a nice looking ass." Almost embarrassingly, I had to agree with her, although I never really thought of my dad's ass as sexy as she called it.

The following day I called Liz to discuss D.D.'s idea: a couple of real cowboys are showing up at a naval function. "It would give these Navy guys something to think about." D.D. flipped a coin to see who would make the all-important call. I lost and had to do the calling. I would do it later in the afternoon and call Liz back with their answer.

Dakota looked at me with her matter of fact voice. She said, "You are a graduate of Annapolis and you are now working on being a jet pilot. We raised you to blaze your trail. Now go forth and ask a couple of cowboys to be your dates!" I had never asked a guy out before; it was always the other way around. So now I was in the hot seat.

I did not find out until many years later, but a couple of mothers were already discussing Liz and me asking John and Robert to the dance. Since D.D. and dad received that late Thanksgiving call and, of course, the once a year Christmas card, our mothers had been secretly communicating with each other.

After dinner I finally went to my bedroom to make the call, where I figured it would be more private. I could hear the dial tone on the other end. It was Robert's mother who answered the phone. We made some small talk, then she said, "You did not call to talk with me; I will get Robert."

Robert came to the phone, which seemed like it took forever. Slowly I requested for both Liz and myself. Amazingly, he agreed to be my date, and then he asked me to wait a minute so he could ask John. It wasn't long before he came back on the phone with John's answer, which was "Yes!" Then we continued with the conversation for another half hour until I remembered that I still had to call Liz.

Liz was three times zones away from us, so it was pretty late there when I called. "It's about time you called. I even tried calling you a few times, and the phone was busy," she complained.

8

NAVY NEW YEAR'S EVE BALL

We met back in San Antonio, with Liz arriving from Washington DC about 3 hours before I arrived. I had promised Robert that I would call him just as soon as I settled back in Kingsville. But of course, the temperature was very different than when I departed Montana. The temperature at the ranch was -20 degrees and here it was 65 degrees. It was an 85 degree difference. Before I made it to the car in the parking lot, I was pealing clothes. Liz was shedding a few herself as she laughed at the oversized parka I was wearing.

We both made sure to call Robert and John that evening. We did not know which one of us had talked the longest with the guys. Between us, we described what the boys should wear for the New Year's Eve ball. The boys asked us what we were wearing, and both of us laughed since we would be wearing our Class A's. The night finally arrived, but not before I called home and my father answered the phone. "Let me talk with D.D., please, Dad, and could you disappear?" He sounded a little surprised but obediently let D.D. have the phone. I started by asking her all sorts of questions about dating and what I should do and pay for since I was the one asking for the date.

There were other questions that only a mother and daughter could communicate. Her last comment was, "I asked your dad out on a date for dinner at my home, and because another man decided to invite himself, the whole date was a disaster. It was always like all the other times in our lives; other guys kept asking themselves into my life. That time I managed to salvage our relationship, and he finally asked me to marry him. You are a beautiful young lady like your mother. So don't worry, just keep other guys at bay and let them know he is your date. Those other guys made me feel like a beautiful girl on the outside; your dad made me feel like a woman on the inside."

New Year's Eve arrived, and both guys showed up at our apartment driving a pickup truck. Both of them looked sharp, and we two ladies would be showing off a couple of cowboys. Both of us offered the use of our cars for the dance, but they declined.

Entering the base gate, both Liz and I had to show our IDs. Then we were on to the building where the dance was taking place. Everything seemed normal until the four of us entered the ballroom. After that, it was a sit-down dinner, and at that time, a few people recognized John who according to the Texas newspaper stories was now news states baseball heroes. Everyone wanted his autograph for their children. Once they finished talking to John, they came over to Robert to wish him luck in reaching the College Baseball's World Series last spring.

Then it was time for the grand entry into the ballroom. Robert rose from his dinner chair and reached out his hand to me asking, "May I have this dance, young lady?" We danced away the evening until the balloons dropped at midnight. Then, like perfect gentlemen, they escorted us back to our apartment. We invited them to come in for a cup of coffee to keep them awake for the drive home. They declined because it was a long way home and they had chores to do in the morning.

At the door Robert smiled at me and said, "I think I had the most beautiful naval pilot there tonight. Thanks for inviting me to join you. It was a special evening. I would like to spend more time with you when you are done and have your wings."

"Thanks for being so considerate of my goals and feelings, Robert," I replied to him. "I think you are someone special also. Let us get together more often if possible." He gave me a beautiful soft kiss, got back into the pickup, and left. All of a sudden, the world felt so empty.

The following day I made a call home, hoping my father was out doing chores. Sure enough, D.D. answered the phone. We must have talked for at least 30 minutes before she said, "Your father is walking up from the barn. Do you want to talk to him?"

I said, "No!" and hung up just as I heard the old screen door slamming shut.

D.D. had said that dad would be heading out on another 10 day trip this afternoon, and she would call back after he left. It was nice talking with her now, knowing more than ever about her relationship with my father. I missed those evenings when I was a little girl, and D.D. would put me to bed. She was my stepmother, but she was also my best friend.

She and my father managed to get away more often with both Mark and me at school. Whenever they came to an event for one of us, they would always make a side trip out of it. Even though she was a cowgirl and loved the outdoors, she managed to take care of herself and always looked sharp.

My father was the same way. Some mornings he still would get out and do a 5-10 mile run. When my father wore his naval uniform or airline uniform, looking sharp was the order of the day. A couple of my former single teachers and many of the flight attendants I had met on the flights when traveling alone always mentioned that he was one of the better-looking and nicer pilots. One of the flight attendants even said, "Your father could put his shoes under my bed any day."

9

PHASE TWO FLIGHT TRAINING

According to my father, the beginning of phase 2 was the most exciting part of the entire program. It would begin with the tactical concepts of different formations, different bombing attacks, and altitude attacks and end in carrier qualifications. Included in this phase was carrier landing practice. The days turned into weeks, and the weeks again turned into months.

There was so much knowledge to learn and more flying than I'd ever done before this time. Still, there was more simulator and class time than my experiences at Annapolis. It was not unusual to burn the mid-night oil if there was time off to do so. Being alert and ready to go in the morning sometimes was difficult. I tried to write or talk to Robert at least once a week. He was busy preparing for graduation and applying to veterinary schools; Pullman, Washington seemed to be the most popular for a good education.

I did have a new PFI after Christmas break, which made me happy. He was very demanding and, best of all, for my purpose, very professional. I was starting to enjoy the learning experience. When

I had a problem, he would run through it several times if need be. It came in handy on the bombing runs and low altitude attacks. Learning specific landing patterns was almost too easy for me since I'd had quite a bit of experience landing at small airports around Montana.

I always wondered why my father was so precise in his landing patterns. Now that I was learning how to land on an aircraft carrier, it finally made sense. He had trained this way, and it had never left him. I made sure Liz and I could talk to him as much as possible when he was home to pick his brain. He was in training a couple of weeks or so every year with the airline, and at the same time, he would be training with the Naval Air Guard out in Washington State. Often I would wonder who was running the farm, but he was also able to spend time there.

It was July, and I was finally doing it all. The only part missing were the carrier operations. We were able to land and take off on a land based carrier before going out to sea. Liz was still with me, but many were dropping out of training. Some of those moved onto other types of aircraft more to their liking. Liz was becoming a lady with no fear. There was nothing that she could not take on with quite a bit of vigor. We pretty much put John and Robert out of our minds for several months. Everything we learned in the last several months was becoming part of the everyday program.

My PFI was always one step ahead of me. I learned that he was one of the best among the maritime fleet community. Liz bragged about her PFI and his patience with her. We often returned to the simulators for practice in our spare time.

Both of us agreed it was the most challenging part of our time together. We would challenge each other continuously as good buddies and good friends. But unfortunately, not many men dared to take us on in training, and when they did and lost, their group razed them about losing to a woman.

When land based carrier landing learning began, I felt comfortable with it the second time on approach and landing. Our family's small landing strip was a good practice one at 78-90 knots. The short landing area was landing at 250 knots and making sure you caught the tail hook before going off the other end.

Both of us managed to catch up with my father before we started the process. He ran us through it via telephone twice in one week: "When you get that down, and they send you out to sea, remember when landing or doing touch and goes, make sure the ship is coming up and meeting the aircraft upon landing."

We spent time in the simulator on our weekends, going over and over it again. Finally, a dozen of us, including Liz and me, were assigned a PFI to teach us the art of meatball, lineup, and the angle of attack. Once that was complete and the PFI felt comfortable enough, we would go out to sea for the final part of our training.

10

CARRIER LANDINGS

The time finally came when we went out to sea. I began to worry about the party afterward! Liz and I were the only two females in the group of males. Just a couple of days before our departure for the aircraft carrier qualification, I called home one more time. This time it would be a woman-to-woman talk. Luckily D.D. answered the phone. I wanted to ask her advice on handling men, especially in a party situation, not then knowing about the case in her life before she became our mother. Just like any group, the rumors would fly about these Golden Wing parties. "You are an officer equal to any man. Don't let them get the upper hand since you both have made it farther than half of your group. Second, your birth mother is looking down on you and is likely very proud of you right now. Lastly, you have one proud father and a stepmother that knows you are one of the best." Her advice was to the point.

I then asked if my father was there. She had replied that he was doing his reserve time before returning home after completing his Asian trip.

I informed her that I had invited Robert and Liz had invited John to the Golden Wing ceremony. Her last comment was, "Take care of yourself and be the lady that your father and I taught you to be. Love you to pieces."

It was early morning when all of the group lined up for takeoff to the aircraft carrier. Just about 3 hours later, we reached the aircraft carrier and started the pattern. Each of us was going to do four touch and goes to get the deck's feel before the final land and catch. We were graded on our landings and touch and goes by our PFIs.

My PFI wanted to make a bet on how I would do for his favorite beverage, so I asked him what his favorite drink was. He not only named his wife's beverage of choice but invited me to dinner with his family. My worry about the party just disappeared. Liz's PFI did the same thing, except she had to make dinner for his family. It was an exciting three days on the ship. Each evening our PFIs reviewed our performance. We toured the big carrier finding our quarters the first night. While touring the ship, we were able to watch a night landing of a Grumman EA6 Prowler.

It was a type of aircraft that had a waiting list for assignments. We noticed as the plane came to a complete halt that Whidbey was on the fuselage. I mentioned to Liz that my father's reserve unit was also Whidbey. Continuing on our way, I never gave a second thought as to why that aircraft was here. We both agreed that its landing was quite beautiful and most likely more professional than any of ours all day.

I hoped my final land and catch would earn the Wings of Gold. I came out of the pattern and lined up with the deck. Relaxed for the first time in three days, I landed my aircraft and my tail hook caught the first cable, coming to an abrupt halt. As I was trying to get back to normal a voice came over the radio, "Congratulations, mister, you are now the second member of the family with Golden Wings."

I could hardly hold my excitement when I recognized my father's voice on the radio. The aircraft we saw doing such a precise landing last night was my father. As I taxied my plane to a designated parking spot, I remembered my conversation with my mother, and the Intruder we saw landing last night. I never even dreamed what my parents were planning. They were always there at Mark's and my special events. My father was not going to miss this one. I finished the check of the aircraft and he came over to my plane and walked with me while I did the final assessment. He advised me that he was returning to Whidbey after the last landing session was over.

I walked with him over to his Intruder. It was a beautiful aircraft and capable of doing almost anything. He had already done his pre-check. Before climbing into the cockpit, he looked back at me and mentioned that he was sorry that D.D. could not make it. Something to the fact that, "She would not fly with me a jet fighter." Liz and her both laughed and watched as his base crew helped him and his weapons control officers get settled into their cockpit.

I returned his salute as he taxied to the main ramp and into the catapult for takeoff. Liz and I were invited to the bridge to watch the process. I was looking at the setting sun as he catapulted off the carrier setting his destination for Whidbey Island Naval Air Station. The whole scene was just like my father loved in real life. Somehow in my heart, I felt he was the setting sun and I would be the rising sun.

The celebration the next evening after returning from the carrier was one of triumph. Liz and I went to our apartment to freshen up before the ceremony to find Liz's parents and D.D. there waiting for us to return.

Liz looked at me with an inquisitive look while we entered our apartment as if I might know something, but I just shook my head "NO." They all previously had arranged to be here and had not informed us. With their mother in toe, Robert and John arrived not much later, giving us little time to get organized. D.D. and Laura were like two long-lost friends meeting each other after so many years.

We let the parents, wives, and even girlfriends pin the new Wings of Gold on the new pilots. D.D. pinned mine on me and then gave me one big hug. "Now," she whispered, "I have two heroes in the family."

I hugged D.D., and I could see a tear in her eye. "Thanks, Mother."

All the parents and guests left and let the party begin for the evening. One of the LSOs asked me if my mother was married. He wished she could have stayed a bit longer so he could spend time with her. "She is beautiful." I smiled to myself, now knowing someone else thought my mother was beautiful.

I gave him a look and asked, "Do you remember that Intruder that left the carrier last night?"

He replied, "Yes, and I saw you were quite friendly with the officer despite you being junior."

"That was my father's Intruder. He came down from Whidbey to make sure I passed my tests."

The PFI smiled and commented to her, "I had dinner with him the evening he arrived. The lead PFI informed us that he was a former Vietnam POW."

I replied to him, "Yes, that is my father."

"Wow! You have good genes. He is a fascinating man, and he also seems very well educated. The PFI that invited him to dinner sparred with him in a training mission a few years back and lost. You must be very proud of him, mister."

"I am," I replied.

It was well after midnight when we finally returned home. Liz's parents were still there, but D.D. had left with John, Robert, and their mother. Liz's parents informed me that D.D. would be staying with them a few days, and Joni's father would most likely fly down and pick her mother up later in the week. It was Saturday morning and there was a note left behind inviting all of us to a Texas barbecue tomorrow afternoon at the Ben's and Laura's family ranch.

We drove out to the ranch early in the afternoon after sleeping in from the late night before. All of the family, including D.D., were there to greet us. Liz's parents had never been to an authentic Texas barbecue before so this was special to them.

When D.D. and I were alone for a short time later in the afternoon, I commented on my conversation with the PFI the evening before: "He was sorry you left so soon after the ceremony was over. The PFI was wondering if you were married; apparently he did not notice the ring on your finger." She just smiled that killer smile of hers.

Sunday evening, I drove over to my PFIs home for dinner bringing along his favorite beverage. I also brought along a bottle of chardonnay for his wife and me. Their three daughters met me at the door.

They escorted me to the kitchen where both he and his wife were preparing dinner. He then introduced me to the whole family—all girls. He explained why he had invited me to dinner: "You see, there are only girls in my family, and I wanted them to meet you. Girls like you set an example for girls like mine. I wanted them to see what you have accomplished, and what they could do if they work hard enough." I just stood there stunned at what I just heard—me, an example!

The rest of the evening was one of finding out about each other. He brought up another subject about his experience on the carrier this past week: "All the PFIs had dinner with an officer the other night from Whidbey. Our lead PFI informed us that he was a Vietnam POW." I just sat there and listened to his admiration for the officer. Then he brought up seeing him meeting my aircraft and watching me walking with him over to his aircraft. "You guys seemed quite chummy for you being a junior and him a captain."

"He is my father," I replied.

"Why didn't you tell me you are a daughter of a naval hero?" he asked.

I replied, "Our parents raised my brother and me to blaze our trails and not ride theirs."

Questioning, he continued, "I was honored enough to meet your mother the night of the ceremony too. She is not only a beauty but also a very interesting lady."

I tried to explain, "She is not my real mother. She is my stepmother. D.D. is an author and writes feel-good stories for a newspaper chain. Unfortunately, my real mother passed away a few months before my father returned from Vietnam."

"I am sorry," he replied to me.

His wife was sitting there with us and joined into the discussion and changed the subject. She was surprised how her husband bragged about this officer he had been training the last several months. "The fact is, I was getting a little jealous since he was spending more time with you than us. But now that I've met you, I can see why he spoke so highly of you. It all changed the other day when he returned home from the carrier, and was telling me about this officer he had dinner with one evening while on the aircraft carrier. So now we know that he has met your whole family."

I interrupted, "Well, you haven't met my brother yet." They all laughed and asked about him. I then explained that my brother was in veterinary school in Washington State and was the only average person in my family! The rest of the evening was one of family, enjoying each other, and making new friends that I would have for the rest of my life.

11

NEXT ASSIGNMENT

It was the start of a new week and month for both Liz and me. First, we put in requests for our dream community locations. We both wanted to stay closer to our family's homes for a while. Then there was the little problem of men. John was finishing out his baseball season in Boston, and Robert was starting veterinary school at Washington State University

Robert and Mark had become friends at WSU and were planning on going home to help our father separate the calves from their mothers and eventually bring them home for the winter. I would have four weeks off before reporting to my new assignment. There was no way I would be able to make it home for the first weekend, but I would be there for the cattle drive.

I requested Lemoore Naval Air Station in California as my first choice and Whidbey Island Naval Air Station in Washington State as my second choice. I wanted to stay on the west coast if possible. My new assignment became my second choice, Whidbey. Liz was going to Naval Air Station Oceana near Virginia Beach, Virginia. I called home, wondering what my father would think about my new assignment. Now the possibility of flying with my father again might happen.

He answered the phone and claimed he had been a bachelor since returning home from his carrier trip. He and the man they had hired had been busy getting ready for winter and preparing for the cattle to come home in a couple of weeks. Mark would be coming home for a few days to help, bringing Robert with him. So they might already be there when arrived. Just like my father to say as an afterthought, "Would you give your boyfriend's parents a call and let your mother know you are ready to leave?"

"Mother is still here?" I asked him. "I thought you were going to fly down and get her."

"Just like a woman, she decided to come with you instead of me. She can change her mind just like anyone else. I am glad she will be coming with you," he kindly mentioned to me.

I had almost forgotten to thank him for coming down and watching me earn my Wings of Gold. When I did, he responded, "I enjoyed it, mister. Just being able to do a night carrier landing again was an exciting exercise. It felt great having dinner with the PFIs the one night we were there. My weapons officer and I had our names on our flight suits blacked out so no one would know who we were except the one officer who was our friend from a previous training exercise, and the commanding officer of the ship, of course."

Just as I hung up the phone, it rang again. Answering, it was John asking for Liz. Instead of giving the phone to Liz, I asked if my mother was handy.

He answered, "Yes, do you want to talk with her?"

"Please," I replied, "just for a few minutes." D.D. answered the phone, "I just heard from Dad that you wanted to ride back home with me."

"Yes," she said. "I decided you need some company. Really, I just want to spend some time with you."

I informed her that I would be out in the morning to pick her up. She then turned the phone over to Liz so she could talk with John.

12

MOTHER AND DAUGHTER ADVENTURE

The following day Liz and I drove our respective cars out to the ranch. Liz was meeting John, who was traveling with her to her parents' home in Virginia. Her parents had just met John for the first time when Liz received her Wings of Gold. They liked John but warned Liz that he might be just a passing flame in the night. He was a baseball player with plenty of females followers. I already knew what my parents thought of Robert, who was coming to the ranch with Mark. I held private thoughts about D.D. wanting to travel with me to Montana; it was going to be an interesting adventure.

We were a few hours into our travels when D.D. finally opened up. She wanted to know how I felt about her and my father's marriage and their relationship. I gave it a deep thought for a minute, then I finally answered.

D.D. had cemented a relationship with Mark and I before she decided to feel comfortable with our father. Although our dad did not show it at first, in the beginning he did not feel comfortable with D.D. being around our family to much at first. I slowly began to pick my words very carefully as I answered D.D.'s question. "I felt my father was very uncomfortable around you at first. Down deep, I feel he really loved our mother and missed her very much. Beginning another relationship, especially with two children, was not in the cards so early after he returned and my mother had passed. You may call it feeling guilty."

D.D. seemed to understand my reasoning. "Your father and I had many long conversations even after he asked me to marry him, and that topic came up often. Before I met you and Mark, your father and I spent a night on that cottonwood stump talking about each other's lives since college, and I felt we both opened up to each other about our feelings. Then I screwed it up by inviting him to dinner, and at the same time, my so-called boyfriend invited himself. He met your father at the door, introducing himself as my fiancéé. Your father left the house that evening very upset and even stopped by a bar in Augusta, running into one of my girlfriends. He walked out on her and just drove home to his haven. I found out about the whole evening just before he left for training in Minneapolis.

"I needed to have a conversation with your father before he again walked out of my life like he did the evening of the senior rodeo party. It seemed like it took me forever to understand that he did not want to be a part of the competition; if I liked him, it was up to me to let him know I cared. I met him at the airport the afternoon before he left for training, and he tried to brush me off with some mean words. I came close to walking off, but tried to understand how he felt after being in prison for four years and losing a loved one. So for the first time in our relationship, I was persistent and stayed the course. We finally departed as friends, although he was still cold up until I let him off at the door of the terminal.

"This might seem odd to you Joni, but I've always been in love with your father. Our problem was other people—mostly other men. They kept coming on to me, and I did not stop them; I likely encouraged them. The day I met your beautiful mother, Eve, and your father at the airport, my whole world fell apart. She told my sister and me that they were planning on getting married and showed us her ring. I liked your mother and was jealous at the same time because she was what every woman wanted to be, and she had the guy that I loved. She was beautiful like you, and intelligent like both you and Mark.

"Both my sister and I could tell your father loved her, even though we just talked to both of them maybe 15 minutes. We could also tell your mother loved him. They seemed to like the same things. The night your grandmother encouraged him to sit down to the piano and play, showed me how much in common and love they shared, and it was beautiful."

"Joni, your mother and I started writing letters to each other after my marriage fell apart and when your father was in prison. Some of our mutual friends from the rodeo team felt it might up lift her spirits. Instead your mother encouraged our spirits. We became closer when my parents were killed. She asked if she could come out and spend a couple of weeks with me. That is when she broke the news to me about her cancer. We laughed and cried those two weeks together. The last thing we did was take an all women pack trip into the backcountry. I still laugh remembering the day she went swimming naked in a cold lake and dared us to follow her. We did. She was extraordinary." Dakota then stopped talking, as if just remembering that day; she seemed lost in thought for the longest time.

We arrived in Albuquerque, New Mexico early afternoon and decided to stay overnight. It was fall, and many of the leaves were still on the trees. The desert laid out its beauty for us. The following day was the beginning of the Balloon Fiesta. Both of us wanted to see at least one day of it. Dakota had been here on business; she knew all the lovely places to shop, eat, and stay.

After 13 months of pressure, I was starting to relax. Being with my stepmother, I finally felt comfortable. She was still writing for a major chain of newspapers and had a couple of books already published. Unfortunately, I had not taken the time to read the books or even watch the movie. She told me much later that our mother-daughter travels had been part of her daily newspaper articles. My father was always proud of her and joined her when she needed him along.

It was hard for me to believe that when we walked into a restaurant, she knew everyone, and they knew her. We ended up with the best table in the house. Her favorite wine was brought to the table. When the waiter asked us what we wanted on the menu, he already knew what D.D. would order. It was like an old friend had come to visit. The waiter even asked about her husband. During dinner, I asked her how was it that everyone knew her. D.D. smiled. "It was two years ago when they were making my book into a movie, your dad and I had some time off so we came down here on location and spent time with all the characters and, of course, the director."

The following day we were up well before sunrise. A shuttle bus stopped by the hotel and transported us to the site where the balloons would take off. It was still dark when we arrived. We could hear mariachi music throughout the gathering site. Somehow D.D. was able to wrangle a ride for both of us in one of the balloons. The group in the balloon began dancing to the music. Finally, the balloons started to lift off into the morning twilight.

It was hard to believe Dakota and I were now in a balloon drifting into the morning sky above the desert. My mother put her arm around me and squeezed hard. "They call it the Dawn Patrol Show," she said. The escalated feeling was something that I had never felt before. It was a freedom to sore high and beyond the sky. The music continued to flow, and all the members in the basket opened a second and third bottle of champagne and toasted the new day.

With D.D. driving, we left Albuquerque early the following day, still excited about our adventure. She began telling me about her relationship with my father. "When your father's contractor called me and asked me to take charge of designing certain areas of the house, I jumped at it. Then your father, you and Mark showed up unannounced that Saturday. Hearing the screen door slam and children laughing, I fell off the ladder and broke the mirror. You came running into the bedroom and scared me to death. Breaking that mirror was supposed to bring seven years of bad luck, but it was good luck for me. I met you and Mark, and life has never been the same since then." We were both laughing just thinking about the first time.

"You see, Joni, I fell in love with you and Mark. It was a feeling that I could not explain at the time. Then I met your grandparents when all of you finally came out to the home your father had us creating for you. Your belongings arrived later and your grandmother and I started helping you put things in order. All of us, including your grandmother, started finding little notes from your mother hidden in both of your treasures. I started to feel another deep connection to your mother and grandparents. Your grandmother and I started to have many mother and daughter talks over many months. She was the one who would make your father marry me if he didn't ask me to. I think your grandfather put the bug into your father's ear."

"Have you ever regretted marrying my father and being our mother?" I asked.

"Not one minute, although I find myself busier than ever holding down a house and trying to write and paint at the same time. Your father encourages me to follow my dreams. He says, 'If you don't, you will always regret it,' and he wants me to be happy, just like last week when he flew down to the carrier to be with you at your special time, and when he manages to be at Mark's special times. He is always there for me, like in Albuquerque, watching my book turn into a movie. His seniority now gives him almost two months off between trips. Somehow he fits his career, reserve time, family, and the ranch into his busy life.

"Last fall, he and I took a pack trip into the Bob Marshall Wilderness by ourselves. We spent one whole week camping, fishing, and just plain talking between ourselves with no outside interruptions. I was getting the feeling that your father will retire shortly from the Naval Reserve. He loves it, but as he says, 'It is time to spent more time at home'."

"Mom, do you think it's dad's PTSD that is keeping him going, or being afraid it just might return if he's not busy?" I asked.

"No, I think it is in his nature. He has always been like that, even when I knew him in high school. He was always busy: doing rodeo, breaking records, and making the team number one.

"One of his friends once told me that he carried a 3.9 grade point average in college. He was on the college swim team, which was not the in thing to do in Montana at the time. I learned later, that to be a Navy fighter pilot, swimming was a requirement. He set a goal and stayed with it."

Cheyenne, Wyoming, was our next stop for the evening. My mother had friends there too; they were planning a dinner together. It would be a girls' night out, but many were bringing members of their families, and I was going to be one of the girls tonight. We talked as we drove through Colorado and into Wyoming.

I began to fill my mother in on the last 13 months of intensive training. I told her about the New Year's Eve ball where Robert and John became the night's hit because of their college baseball and football. We laughed together about the Navy officer attracted to D.D. on the final night when I received my Wings of Gold. He had already approached D.D. and wanted her to stay for the party. She politely informed him that it was her daughter's party and not her's. Before leaving, D.D. thanked him for the invite. They laughed when I informed him later that he had dinner with her husband the evening before on the carrier.

Cheyenne was in the window, and New Mexico and Colorado were in the rearview mirror. My stepmother had talked with one of her friends in Wyoming just before we had begun our travels. They had planned a gathering for us for when arrived in Cheyenne. One of them had made dinner reservations in a private room for the party.

When we arrived at the hotel, the party was already in progress. We decided to go to our room, freshen up a bit, and call home. Mark and Robert were at the ranch and had worked all day gathering cattle, doctoring cattle, and shipping most of the calves out. The men were sitting down to dinner when D.D. called. They all sounded tired, but she did not talk very long, knowing that I wanted to talk to Robert. It did not take D.D. very long to comb her hair and put on some makeup. Then, leaving the room, she motioned to me that she would meet me down in the lobby for dinner after I talked to Robert.

I did not talk to Robert very long, knowing that he was probably very tired. Our father had a habit of putting people to work that came to visit. However, I did find out that Mark and Robert would stay for the weekend so I could spend a few days with him when I arrived. Hanging up, I proceeded down to the hotel's lobby for the party.

People were standing around everywhere, most holding a drink or a glass of wine. D.D. never really explained to me how these people became friends or knew her. Some of them seemed to be a tag-along that came with someone who was a friend. Everyone finally settled down to dinner and instead of sitting with my mother, I sat next to a young man about my age or a little older.

We made small talk before introducing ourselves. His name was Roger and he informed me that he was a doctor in Cheyenne. His received medical degree was from the University of Cleveland. He had done his internship in Cleveland before returning to Wyoming. I asked him if he was happy to be back home and practicing medicine. His face lit up and he said, "They needed a doctor here, and the government would pick up my student loan if I returned and practiced in the community. Patients are just starting to adjust to this kid they all watched grow up in Cheyenne now being their doctor."

He described his practice here in Cheyenne. Most of his patients knew him, and he knew them. His background in medical school and during his internship was in surgery, which it seemed he had done a lot of lately. Farm accidents were the worst, and he had lost a few patients, including a best friend from high school.

His mother had conned him into coming tonight by saying, "You might meet some nice young lady that wants to marry a doctor."

I looked right in his eyes and asked, "Well, have you met some nice young lady tonight?"

He was embarrassed when I put the question to him. He shyly and embarrassingly replied, "Yes, I have, and it has been an interesting experience."

I replied, "Well, I guess mothers know best, don't they?" All he could do was agree with my statement.

The conversation got around to me. He asked, "So what about you? Are you still in college working for your degree?"

I replied, "I am an Annapolis Naval graduate with a bachelor's degree in chemistry and a master's degree in physics, and just this last week I earned my Wings of Gold.

"Wow!" It was hard to tell whether he was impressed or not when he asked, "What does it mean when you earn your Wings of Gold?"

Smiling, she gave him a wicked look. "The Wings of Gold means I am a Navy fighter pilot."

"Do you land on aircraft carriers too?"

"Yes, I do."

"All of sudden, me being a doctor isn't as impressive as I thought it was."

I tried to reassure him that his chosen profession was essential. The rest of the evening as we discussed both of our professions, I couldn't help comparing him to Robert.

Our conversation led to the party, as I wondered how my mother knew all of these people. Roger, who sat beside me most of the evening, was surprised that I did not know who they were. So he set out to explain: "These ladies are rodeo friends of your mother and my mother. Most of them competed in high school and college rodeo together. A few, like your mother, went onto the professional RCA circuit. Your mother married a professional cowboy and left it when her parents offered them a down payment on a ranch for their wedding. Dakota's parents died in an automobile accident shortly after she was married. All of these people here came together at their funeral to support her. They are rodeo buddies, and they come together to celebrate their friendship. Not all of them are from Wyoming; some are from Colorado and Montana."

Roger continued, "They get together once a year. Besides that, your mother is famous because of her book telling the story of women in rodeo. Your father left the circuit when he joined the Navy, but many others from those college ranks kept going. It gets into your blood, and Dakota's first husband was one of those men. I heard my parents say that he was an alcoholic and played around even after they were married. When he was home and drunk, my mother said he that would beat your mother."

I felt a sinking feeling of shock from what Roger was telling me. My stepmother never discussed her previous marriage. Right now, this was her life, and she let everyone, including her stepchildren, know that she loved it.

Roger and I continued to discuss our professional lives. He seemed very interested in why I would pick such a profession as a woman. I told Roger that I fell in love with flying because of my father. "He even came down from Washington with his Intruder and showed all of us how easy it is to land on a carrier. I did not know it was him until my last landing when he came on the radio and congratulated me for earning my Wings of Gold." Roger and I exchanged addresses and promised to keep in touch with each other.

The following day as the sun was rising over the Wyoming high country, D.D. and I were on our way north to Montana. She questioned me about my evening with a specific doctor that was with his mother at the gathering. I smiled and informed her that I had an interesting discussion and he was a great dancer. "I discovered quite a bit about you last night. I did not realize that you stayed in rodeo after dad left for the Navy and that you even married a professional cowboy."

"Joni, now that you are an adult, did you ever wonder why your dad and I never had any children other than the two of you?" D.D. took a few breaths, either waiting for an answer or just wondering what to say next. "After your dad asked me to marry him, he and I had a long discussion, and I told him why I could never have any more children. We were out in the barn putting the horses to bed one evening when we sat down in the tack room. It was still winter, and your grandmother, whom I confided in, encouraged me to have a conversation with your father."

"My ex-husband had a habit of getting drunk and beating me. One time he kicked me in the stomach with his boots. I was pregnant with his child he did not want. He beat me so badly that I lost the baby. The doctor told me that he had done so much damage that I would never have another child. I was in the hospital for a few days then came home. I filed charges against him, and he spent six months in jail. Before I left the hospital, one of the ladies you met last night was married to an attorney. He managed to get a restraining order against him and file for divorce at the same time. He was banned from the RCA circuit completely; I never heard from him again after the divorce. One of the ladies last night mentioned he was somewhere in Nevada working as a cowhand for some large ranch."

"That night in the barn's tack room, I finally told your father the story. He stood there silently for the longest time. The fact he stood there so long scared me. I was sitting there thinking this was the end of a great dream. He then walked over and put his arms around me and said, 'We have two children to raise, and that was your life in the past, just like my prison. It is time for both of us to move on with our lives. I love you. The children love you, so the only choice is letting the past go and move on together.'."

"Joni, do you remember when I loaded you and Mark into the car, and we drove to Washington State to be with your father?"

I replied that I did. My mother then again asked, "Do you remember a man that sat down and talked to all of us the last evening we were there?" Again I replied that I did. Once again, D.D. started speaking, "Your father and I have had many conversations with him over the years alone and together."

Then it was my turn, "Mother, he was one of the three psychologists that interviewed me when I was in Florida." My statement surprised her. I continued, "He told me, just before I was dismissed from the room, to tell both of you that Phil said, 'Hi!' He also said that you were a fascinating couple and he has enjoyed talking to you over the years."

"Your father spent several more days with him and over the phone in conversation. One day, Phil called to talk with your father who was out in the field. I asked if I could take your father's time. He said that he was willing to discuss anything with me." That began many discussions over the years with your father and me separately and together. He has become a friend to both of us even though he did not name us in a book that he wrote about our family's experience with PTSD.

"Now that you know my history, let's discuss you and your life," D.D. very nicely changed the subject to me. "Let us hope your life isn't filled with as much drama as mine has been. When I met your mother, all I could think of was her being beautiful and outgoing. Since graduating Annapolis, you've met two sharp-looking guys that I know of, and both of them seem very much attracted to you."

I tried to answer the question as best as I could about the two guys that seemed to be attracted to me. "I like both of them, but one needs to finish school, and the other one needs to marry someone from his hometown instead of me. I believe he would feel the pressure of trying to keep up with me as many males do. Robert takes one day at a time and realizes we both have goals in our lives which we want to accomplish. So as he says, 'Let us take our time and see where it goes.' I like his outlook on life in general. The Navy has me for the next six years, and until then, I am theirs. Fellow officers don't do it for me. I am not too crazy about dating Navy guys since I am one. I've had a few ask me for dates in school and training, and I have gone out with some of them, but for some reason, I am not attracted to them like other women are these days."

13

HOME BETWEEN ASSIGNMENTS

We had passed Billings, Montana by mid-day. Getting closer to home felt good. Three weeks at home for this Navy girl, and I would enjoy it as long as my father let me rest somewhat. They both knew that the following weekend would be a cattle drive home. When D.D. talked to her father last night, he mentioned that the wheat was being hauled out in large semis for markets on the Columbia River in Washington State. The calves had already left earlier for feedlots in Central Washington.

    I loved to fly. The feeling of that much power beneath me was exhilarating. D.D. asked many questions about my training and the time I had spent at Annapolis. She mentioned that both she and my father had tears in their eyes when they left me at Annapolis my freshman year. When I came home during Christmas break, I was a woman instead of a girl. My father commented, "She grew up too fast."

    "The Academy called about two months before graduation and asked him to say a few words on graduation day, and they also asked him to present the diplomas." Dakota said, "He felt honored and humbled at the same time. A state university graduate instead of an Annapolis graduate; your father was nothing but an ordinary Montana cowboy fresh off the range when he entered the Navy. He always felt that he did not deserve to be among the elite of the Navy. Even when he returned home, it was hard for him to accept the special treatment people bestowed on him."

I had all the credentials of an actual Navy fighter pilot. An Annapolis graduate master's degree, a Navy father, and now I was a real fighter pilot. The only problem was that I was a female who had to prove myself even more than the men. My mother and I spent much of the travel time discussing how I would circumvent that obstacle. Life for a woman in today's Navy wasn't going to be easy.

During our time at the Academy, both Liz and I were never encouraged to follow our dream. Many of the male pilots that were teaching discouraged us from even trying. We not only made it, but many times out matched the men in the same classes.

I enjoyed being with my stepmother and was glad that she decided to return to Montana with me. Shortly after we drove through Great Falls and made our way north and northwest towards the Rockies, I wanted her to know I enjoyed having the company and the adventures we both shared.

Shyly, I turned towards D.D. and let her know in a slow, calculated way, "Mother, thanks for making this trip the most memorable I've ever had. I could not have asked for a better stepmother than you. You were there when I started finding notes from my mother and you made sure I kept them. You put those notes in a book for me to enjoy for my whole life, and maybe share with my children. I still can remember the night you came into my room and found me crying and understood; it was so special to me. Like you, I still talk with my mother. Before catching the first cable, I talked to her about the last landing on the carrier. Then my father coming on the radio afterward made me so proud of both of you. You have been the best parents any girl would like to have. Thank you for being you."

D.D. gave me an appreciative look. "Your father gives your mother credit for taking the rough edges off of a cowboy and making him a gentleman. I knew him in both lives. I feel both of their influences have most likely rubbed off on me. I was so lucky to end up with your small family in many ways. Your grandparents have always been special to me over the years.

"Your grandparents and your father encouraged me to make a life outside of my family responsibilities. Even though sometimes my husband and I miss each other, it still brings us together, knowing we both have something to contribute to our family and each other. It has been fun and exciting the last 17 years."

As the Sawtooth Ridge came into view, my heart started to beat just a little bit faster in anticipating meeting Robert after so long a separation. There were lights on in the house as we drove up and parked. The minute we got out of the car, we could smell food in the air. Stretching and walking into the home, the smell was more robust—steak, potatoes and corn on the cob. While two apple pies sat cooling on the stove, Mark and my father were in the kitchen working away. Robert and a young lady were seated in a couple of chairs admiring the work the men were doing. Seeing Mark's mother and sister arriving, the young lady immediately rose from the chair and walked over to us. She introduced herself as Judy, a friend of Mark's. Judy indicated that she was also a student of the veterinary school.

D.D. took one look at the goings-on in the kitchen, and then commented, "You must be a pretty smart young lady. Relaxing with a glass of wine, watching two men cooking dinner. Let us know how you managed to do this, would you."

Judy laughed and remarked, "Mark always tells me that he has the most incredible stepmother in the world. Actually I was able to bake the pies earlier today."

We all laughed, and my father yelled at them, "Dinner is ready. Come and get it or forever hold your peace." I knew that I was home, and all I wanted to do was sit down and be a family for one evening. It was life from another busy day on the Eastern Front of the Rockies.

The following morning it was still dark over the plateau when D.D. and I started breakfast. At the same time, everyone else was getting the horses ready for the ride to the pasture. The newly hired hand and his wife volunteered to have lunch prepared at the halfway point. After that, they would return the horse trailer and the range rider's camper to the ranch.

The range rider was a young teacher from Spain named Leonardo. He had come over to work on his thesis and watch the cattle like Bernhard had done before him. Bernhard was his professor and suggested that he might complete it working for my father. So he did, and would be returning to Spain in a few days. While here and working in solitude, he fell in love with the country and promised to return next year if asked. His last duty was today when he was going to help trail the cattle home.

He had met Mark a few times through the summer, but he had never met me. Right off, he was attracted to me, but he also noticed that I seemed to be with Robert. Throughout the day, we talked some during the drive. During lunch, we all spoke about college, and caught up on our lives over the last couple of years.

I was able to converse somewhat with him in Spanish as I had taken Spanish in high school, and again at the Naval Academy. While in Texas, Liz and I often visited a Mexican restaurant to brush up on our Spanish. Everybody, including Robert, felt I was showing off my language skills. So, like a brave Spanish gentleman, Leonardo asked for my address, and managed to slip his to me in Spanish. Somehow the only person that understood or figured out what was happening was D.D. When riding together during the cattle drive, my mother very nicely let me know she knew what was happening.

We all arrived home tired and hungry with some 400 head of cattle. The large dining room table easily accommodated all of us. Everyone enjoyed the evening before Mark, Robert and Judy returned to school the following day. My father would fly Leonardo to Great Falls, where he would catch a flight to the East Coast and then onto his home country.

Sometime after everyone went to bed, D.D. asked her husband, "Why don't you let Joni fly Leonardo to Great Falls tomorrow morning instead of you?"

Larry gave her a strange look and knew what was going through his wife's mind. A smile and a slow, "All right."

The group returning to school was off at the first light of day after a hearty breakfast. I immediately asked my father if I could go with him and Leonardo to Great Falls. He gave me a strange looked and answered back with a smile, "Why don't you just take him yourself?" I did not even hesitate after that. I just went over to pre-check the airplane and made sure everything was up to snuff.

Larry handed Leonardo a paycheck for the summer. Then Leonardo asked Larry, "Does Joni know how to fly such a difficult airplane?"

My father smiled and replied, "Don't let her hear you say that, or you will get the ride of your life. Just get in, sit down and watch; let her fly the airplane."

D.D. and my father were standing at the takeoff pad waving goodbye as I taxied the plane onto the runway and started the takeoff towards the Sawtooth Ridge. In Spanish, Leonardo said "beautiful" as he watched the Eastern Slope of the Rockies out of the aircraft windows as we slid by them on our way to Great Falls.

Right after the takeoff, D.D. remarked to her husband, "What I wouldn't give to be a fly in that airplane right now without those two knowing it."

Her husband just gave her a strange look and replied, "Women!" He then started off to do the morning chores.

For Larry, it had not only been a busy week, but a busy month, with Joni receiving her wings, weaning the calves from their mothers, doctoring and pregnancy testing the cattle, shipping the calves and getting the wheat off to the international terminals. He was happy to be relieved of a chore that would have killed 4 or 5 hours out of his day. Knowing that Joni was delighted to do it was just fine with him. Just as long as she did not bring Leonardo back, it was alright.

My passenger and I landed in Great Falls safely, despite Leonardo's worry about a woman flying the airplane. I taxied up to the aviation terminal and watched the flagger as he directed me into a parking spot. I looked over at my passenger, who was hanging onto his bookcase like a life vest.

I laughed and said with a smirk, "You are not used to a woman flying an airplane, Leonardo. Let us get out and have the aviation company take us over to the passenger terminal."

"Can we walk?" Leonardo asked.

"Sure," I replied. It was maybe 1/2 mile over to the terminal, but we walked, with Leonardo pulling his roller bag behind him and his book bag on top. He wanted to let me know that he would like to know me better, if that was possible.

Seriously I replied, "You do know that I am a Naval officer, don't you?" He nodded, wondering what was going to come out next. "I am also a Navy fighter pilot."

He gave that Spanish smile she had learned to like in the last couple of days or so. "I will be a professor in a few months if that makes any difference. Your beauty is that of the mountains I just left behind. Your personality is that of a brilliant lady. Since we are so far apart, can we write to each other? Just maybe your family will let me come back next year."

"I love to write letters," I replied in a matter-of-fact voice. It seemed like wherever I went, there was a man who wanted to know me. On our travels from Texas to Montana, D.D. had said that I had the beauty of my mother.

Life for me slowed down somewhat for a couple of weeks while I was at home. I was either outside helping my father or inside helping my mother. Then there were days when D.D. would be in the den typing away. She always worked with some relaxing music. I would often go out and sit on El Tocon and listen as nature took over the moment. Many times a deer would join me, or an owl would listen to my thoughts.

My stepmother had already informed me she would ride with me to Whidbey Island Naval Air Station in Washington State and help me get settled. The next several months would include much more training on the EA-6B Prowler. My father had been flying the aircraft for some time and liked it. One of the evenings at dinner, he mentioned that he might retire since it was getting harder to continue the training at the Naval Air Station.

He had moved from co-pilot to captain when Mark and I started high school. When he made captain, he began flying out of Minneapolis, making it harder to keep up with his Naval Reserve training. However, he loved Seattle and the crew based there. Just before I entered flight school, he returned to Seattle and seemed happier.

14

WHIDBEY ISLAND NAVAL AIR STATION

The time finally came, and I had to leave for Whidbey. Once getting me settled, D.D. would join my father in Seattle on his Asian trip. They would be spending some quality time together, even if the crew was along. D.D. and I left early in the morning as the sun started rising over the plateau. Dad made breakfast for us and packed a lunch to eat along the way.

It was sad when we left the ranch and set our destination for Whidbey. We had a lot of work to do there after I checked in with the base, hopefully that same evening. The best part was that my father was still based there in the reserves, so he gave me some good advice.

We arrived on base after dark and the guard at the checkpoint directed us to the temporary housing. The following day, I reported to the base training offices. "We were expecting you, mister," a training officer welcomed me. He indicated that they had a few more new training officers arriving within the next couple of days. In addition, he gave me the phone number of another female officer looking for a roommate. She was a P-3C lead who had been stationed here since arriving from Guam.

I made the call to the officer, and she answered right away. She gave me directions to her apartment so my mother and I would not get lost. We found the apartment very attractive, and the officer was not only helpful, but friendly. Her name was Betsy, and she had been based here for two years. Betsy helped us unload the car and move into my new quarters; it was still early when the we finished up the process.

D.D. offered to buy everyone an early dinner before she figured out a way to return to Seattle, eventually meeting her husband. He had informed D.D. that there was an air porter service from the base to the Seattle-Tacoma Airport. He had used it enough in the last several years. Betsy also knew where to catch the service, so she phoned and made reservations for D.D.

We ate at an off-street cafe recommended by my father, with the best seafood stew that all of us had ever tasted. D.D. was surprised by how well her husband ate while he was on reserve duty for the Navy. It was her turn to razz him when she finally met him in Seattle. This place was beyond incredible, but still relatively small with the best seafood she had ever tasted.

When the time arrived, we all went to where D.D. would catch the shuttle to Seattle-Tacoma airport. Hopefully, it could drop her off at the hotel where she was planning to meet my father. When she boarded the shuttle, the shuttle driver asked her name, "Finally, I meet the lady that is married to Larry Becker." D.D. gave him a look that would kill most guys! Then she remembered that her husband had most likely ridden this shuttle many times.

The time seemed to pass very slowly as she took out one of her manuscripts to read along the way. She was looking out the windows as the shuttle passed along the freeway and noticed the fall colors were starting to show. Although Larry always talked about the Pacific Northwest, she seldom had a chance to join him out here. His time was always for doing his duty with the Navy and then returning home. That duty usually happened after completing one of his trips to Asia.

I finally settled into my new home. Betsy and I ended up being like two peas in a pod. Once in a while Liz and I would talk to each other about our new training schedule. It seemed like training was going to be one endless program. However, it was a different program every day, and once a week, flying in the same type plane that my father was flying when doing his reserve duty.

The training was the same as in Texas. The only difference was the change of aircraft. Betsy had transferred with the P-3C Orion squadron from Guam to Whidbey. There were more females in that squadron than the one I was now assigned. I had no intention of flying the P-3C.

I had my heart was set on the Prowler, and I wanted to be the pilot and not the weapons control officer. Each new day brought a new challenge, which I enjoyed. It kept my attention and brains working at warp speed.

Once a week we practiced landing on a carrier; once a month doing the actual landing. When Betsy and I were off the same days, we would explore around the island. Many times we found new places to shop and eat other than on the base. Even the male officers in the training and regular groups started to join us on our search. Those who joined us became our friends, and passing information about the activities and shopping was a typical conversation each time we got together.

15

MY FATHER'S LAST MISSION

Mark, Robert and Judy arrived for Thanksgiving. It was a pleasant surprise, and they joined our little group of officers for Thanksgiving dinner. Both Betsy and I managed to put together a surprising dinner for all. The small apartment rang with constant change through the holiday weekend. Many single males knew this was the place to come for a great home cooked meal, especially during the holiday weekend. I felt proud, showing my brother and Robert around the base. Friday, the squadron decided to put on a little show for all the families with a couple of fly byes.

Both Mark and I wondered where our parents were spending the day. Since our father had been on one of his regular flights to Asia, Mark remarked that he thought they most likely would be in New York City for a layover before returning to Asia and home.

Unannounced, my parents arrived on base Saturday morning. The sun was just rising when the doorbell rang. Betsy was the first there and opened the door still half asleep. Standing before her were an airline pilot and D.D. She half embarrassedly invited them in and offered cups of coffee. "Joni, your mother is here with some sharp-looking airline pilot she must have picked up on her adventures," Betsy called to me. Both of my parents smiled just a little bit at the remark. Betsy had met D.D. when I had moved in, and fell in love with her from the beginning.

I finally appeared from my bedroom only to be met by a statement from my father, "I understand you are going to be in the right seat this afternoon." I gave him a strange look wondering whether to believe him or not. "We are reporting at 1200, so you better get going. You will be flying with your father for the first time, mister." He wasn't kidding, and Betsy, standing there in shock, could not even say a word. I had flown the aircraft a few times with a trainer onboard, but this would be a first with my father.

It just wasn't my father and I when we reported to the flight operations office. There were going to be three other Prowlers joining us with my father as the leader. We were going to fly north along the American and Canadian coasts to Alaska. Halfway into the mission an air tanker would meet us. I had never experienced a fueling operation before. The total time would be 6 hours. Before the mission started, my father had announced his retirement from the service— this would be his last mission. It was all a complete surprise for me.

My parents had already made the decision before his carrier appearance for my Wings of Gold flight. Sadly, this would be our first and only time as father and daughter flying together as Naval officers. We did the pre-check and pre-flight checks together before being helped by personnel into the cockpit. One of the personnel smiled and saluted my father as he assisted him with harness and helmet. He said, "Sir, it has been a pleasure knowing you; we all wish you the best. We will take special care of your daughter now."

My father saluted him and said, "Thanks for the memories."

Then all four Intruders taxied out to the runway per instructions of the base tower. I read the checklist before takeoff as my father answered promptly. Then two jets at a time took off racing down the runway and climbing into the afternoon air. An air of excitement and emotion ran through my blood and nerves. I went through the weapons checklist as I did in training, while my father signaled to the other crews who had joined us at the beginning of the mission. Then, out across Puget Sound and the San Juan Islands into the Straits of Georgia. Clouds beneath us and the sun and blue sky above us, each Prowler held positions in the V.

Their mission took them over the Hecate Strait into the Gulf of Alaska. Just before reaching Alaskan airspace, a call from the tanker came notifying the squadron of its position. Each aircraft set its automatic pilot towards that position. It was about 15 minutes later when the tanker came into view. Our plane would be the first to go in for refueling. When completed, each aircraft would back away and let another aircraft move in for the operation.

The refueling operation was a first for me as I watched from the right seat. These pilots were reserve officers, but each one operated with the professionalism of a regular Naval officer. They'd been around from either Vietnam or shortly after the war. Two of them, including my father, flew for an airline. One was a medical doctor; the other was an engineer for the local aircraft company. As for my father, this would be his final mission. As the aircraft moved away from the tanker, my father thanked them for coming out on the weekend. Then returning to the formation, the small group proceeded back to Whidbey.

My father advised the other three to land first, and then we took one final pass over the airfield. "Someday, you will be doing this, and I hope I will be around to experience again what I'm experiencing now," he commented. D.D., Betsy, Mark, Judy and Robert were waiting as we taxied up to the hangar. We followed the flagger as we parked our aircraft and did our paperwork. The canopy opened and the aircraft maintenance personnel started taking command of the plane. My father and I made one last check of the aircraft as D.D. came over gave him a big hug and kiss that seemed to last forever, as if she was glad to have him back again. Robert gave me a bigger hug and kiss than at the New Year's ball in Kingston. He did not hold back for the first time in our relationship which began Thanksgiving a year ago at his parents' home in Texas.

The reserve squadron had a gathering ready for my father when we entered the debriefing room of the hangar. He gave a very short, "Thank you for everything." He and D.D. stayed around for a short time and then left with our family in tow.

Our family went to my father's and now mother's favorite seafood restaurant and enjoyed another great meal. I was seeing, as an adult, my parents caring for each other and their children. Deep down in my heart, I had a dream that I would have the love they had between them one day. I remembered after they were married, my parents often visited the old cottonwood stump down by Willow Creek and enjoyed a fire. I noticed when I was home the last time that it still was being used once in a while.

They left late in the evening, returning to Seattle to catch an early morning flight home. It felt lonely without the enthusiasm both of them transmitted. Sunday morning, Mark, Judy, and Robert left early enough to make it back to Eastern Washington by evening. Come Monday morning, it felt strange being in training after the Saturday afternoon adventure I had with my father. Just as I thought back on the carrier, watching him leave that evening returning to Whidbey, he was now definitely the sun's setting, and I would be the rising of a new day.

Having Robert meet me Saturday evening after we had completed our mission and then giving me the biggest hug and kiss made me feel wanted. It was hard to calculate his feelings. He encouraged and sometimes offered advice when he understood what I was doing. But I seemed to understood his goals so much more than he did mine. He and Mark had become good friends in school and had helped each other along in their studies. Yet something was missing from our relationship that I could not put a finger on.

The training was similar to the training I had in Kingston. The only exception was a different aircraft and one that had more power behind it. My father made flying in formation easy when I flew with him and his fellow pilots. I ended up being on the wing most of the time. The weapon delivery system was very different than in the aircraft had I trained in earlier, and landing it on a carrier was even more complex than when I'd earned my wings.

Liz enjoyed her assignment but found the same problems with being a female in her Naval program. The weather on the East Coast was much different than on the West Coast. Liz was excited to hear of my experience with my father. The refueling operation that I experienced with him was one neither of us had a chance to do yet. My father had been doing this for many years and he did his job with great professionalism. Everyone that knew him respected him for the man he was. I was hoping that one day I could be like him.

16

CHRISTMAS LEAVE

The days turned into weeks and the weeks turned into Christmas. My father went back to work right after Thanksgiving so he could manage to have Christmas off. He had made reservations for me from Seattle to Great Falls. I was a big girl, so flying on his airline passes became only dreams of past travels. When I checked in at the gate in Seattle, everyone knew whose daughter I was. Robert decided to return to Texas for Christmas with his family. He had more time off than I did, and I agreed with him that family was important. Besides, as he said, the weather in Texas was much warmer than in Washington or for that matter, Montana.

When I boarded the plane, the airline personnel had assigned me an aisle seat. However, a last minute company employee boarded the flight and ended up taking the center seat. He was still in uniform as an airline pilot, so I presumed he worked for the airline. I felt sorry for him, crammed into the middle seat and trying to stuff his flight bag and suitcase away. Finally, with both of us settled, he introduced himself. His name was Jim Evanston, and he was going to Billings, a stop after Great Falls. His parents owned a ranch in Central Montana. It was going to be his first Christmas home in many years.

Since both of us were in uniform, we pretty much knew what each other did for a living. Jim was a co-pilot for the airline on the 747, and as he put it, "the junior puke."

Then he took note of my Navy Class A's and asked me what I did for the Navy. Even though I was proud of my standing, I sometimes was afraid of letting people know what I did. "I am training on the A-6 Prowler right now. Hopefully I will be done by February."

Instead of being impressed with what I did, he asked me how I liked the aircraft and how far along in training I was.

"Are you Larry's Becker's daughter?" he finally asked. I was not really surprised since my father also flew for the same company and also out of Seattle.

"Yes," I said.

"Wow! Your father and I fly together once in a while. But unfortunately, he has more seniority than I do. His co-pilots are high seniority also, so I don't get very many flights with him."

The conversation turned personal after we became more familiar with each other. Jim had just purchased a home in Everett, Washington. Like me, he dated once in a while, but his life was hectic at the moment. Plenty of airline single ladies had invited him over for dinner. Once in a while, he attended airline employees gatherings, but nothing serious.

I said kind of the same thing, except it was only one guy, Robert. Somehow, I felt no sparks were there like my dad and birth mother had, and now my father and stepmother had. He decided to go home to Texas for Christmas and would not be back to school until sometime after New Year's. "I think my father worked him too hard the time he came out to the ranch," I said, smiling.

"When are you returning to Whidbey after Christmas?" he asked.

"I report back at to base on the 27th," I answered.

"Don't you have a New Year's Eve dance?" he asked.

"Yes, I have never really thought of it or of going. My roommate is going with an attorney she has been dating for a while. Thought I would stay home and study."

He smiled at her the best he could, cramped into the center seat where he could hardly breathe. "How would you like me to escort you to the dance? I am a pilot just like your father, and we work for the same airline. I am from Montana like you are as well."

We had just landed in Great Falls when he presented the offer to me so I had little time to think about it. "I would like that, but could we have dinner before we go? My father found a great seafood place near the base. I want to go there if you are up to it." He dug a piece of paper out of his bag, wrote his phone number on one side, and tore it off, giving it to me. I then wrote my name and phone number on a piece I tore off the bottom of it. "Do you need any other information?" I asked while the plane was pulling into the gate.

"Just your address and I will pick you up at 5 PM if that is all right." I gave him my address and proceeded to stand up from my seat and retrieved my carry-on bag from the overhead compartment. He finally stood up and stretched his cramped legs out, reaching for the ceiling. "See you New Year's Eve at 5 PM," he commented.

I could not believe what I had just done. A guy I hardly knew had asked me out on a date for the Navy New Year's dance and I had said yes. I was thinking to myself that he was good-looking in his pilot's uniform. It was an exciting flight over and the conversation was interesting. Finally, I was talking with someone who seemed interested in my profession.

My father and D.D. were waiting for me when I exited the jet way. He immediately took my carry-on from me and carried it to the baggage claim area. The afternoon drive was just like many Christmases before this one; snow on the ground and the temperature hovering below freezing. The sun was out and the skies of Montana were clear. Even the Rockies were displaying all their wonders as we drove towards the ranch.

I was still confused about my reaction towards a guy I hardly knew on the airplane. He seemed to know quite a bit about the dance and how the Navy operated. I did not know if I should tell my father about the guy I had accepted a date with. My father knew him, but only as a part of a crew. I wasn't even sure that he was single like he said. He had no ring on his finger and was going home for Christmas with his family, not somebody else's.

I knew my mother was counting on Robert joining the family, but I wasn't sure about him. None of the guys I had met lately really did it for me. I always had a distinct feeling, wondering if a female fighter pilot could even fit into ordinary life. Most males in the Navy were just friends. I felt most male Naval personnel usually married someone outside of the Navy. The men on the outside would ask me to give up my career and stay home—I would have none of that.

Christmas was family time, with family arriving for Christmas dinner. D.D. and my father usually worked on the meal together. Dads, brothers, sisters, their almost grown children and Dakota's small family most always joined us for Christmas. Cousins galore was the norm these Christmases in our home.

I could always tell my parents were proud of their children. My father always bragged about me graduating from the Naval Academy and my brother attending veterinary school at Washington State

University. But my mother and father never bragged about their own lives. My father was one of a kind, and so was my stepmother. Never once in the whole day did my father mention that he had just retired from the Naval Reserve; never once did D.D. mention that her new book had just been published. Both of them were great listeners. D.D. had once said that is how you get stories.

Dinner was always the same, with some talk about what was happening around the ranch or about some new machine my dad had purchased to make ranch chores more manageable. So much had changed over the years with automation; it used to take two people to feed the cattle twice a day during the winter, but now it took only one. That one was always in a heated cab while doing it. It used to take two mowers to mow the hay during the summer; now, my father had one machine that took only one person and did three times more mowing. My father worked two jobs so he could purchase most of the equipment. He was flying for the airline, had been flying for the Navy and was still ranching on top of all that.

Everyone left after the early afternoon dinner. Then it was only Mark and me with our parents. We sat down in front of the fireplace and just relaxed. Our father had his only drink of the year. My mother and I were enjoying a glass of wine while Mark went for a hot buttered rum.

It was a time to catch up on each other's lives over the last couple of months. Mark brought up his relationship with Judy. D.D. asked him about Robert, who he said was a good guy but didn't know much about his life outside of school. I was interested in how Robert had been after Thanksgiving. My brother felt Robert might change his courses for the next semester.

Mark was happy with his grades and how school was progressing. His relationship with Judy mainly involved studying. They had rented an apartment together. Both of them were majoring in the same course of study.

I was a little afraid to speak up when D.D. asked me about the upcoming Navy New Year's Eve dance. "Do you have a date, or are you even thinking of going?"

Then, taking a long breath, I shyly asked my dad, "Dad, do you know Jim Evanston?"

"Yes, he is a junior co-pilot on the whale. We've had a few flights together. I believe he is from Montana. He mentioned that his parents have a ranch near Roundup. Why do you ask?"

"He is my date to the Navy New Year's Eve dance this year. He and I ended up sitting next to each other on the flight from Seattle."

My father looked at me with that poker face he puts on once in a while. "I can't tell you much, except he is a good pilot. When I last saw him, he was buying a home near Everett. I know that he is flying reserve these days. He asked you?"

"Yes," I replied.

"Enjoy yourself and let us know how the evening turns out."

I returned to base two days after the long weekend. I did some simulator training and just plain studying for the next part of my training. Jim called twice to see how I enjoyed the long weekend in Montana. Each time we had conversations that lasted for a long time. Not once did he ask about what he was supposed to wear for the evening. Instead, I mentioned to him that I was wearing my Class A's. It left me wondering what it would be like at Whidbey with a civilian dress male. The evening finally came; he found his way to our apartment. Betsy had left earlier with her date for dinner and the dance later.

Standing at the door with a dozen roses, Jim rang the doorbell. When I opened the door, there stood one sharp-looking Naval officer in a uniform which outranked mine. I did not know whether to salute or what. My mouth stood open just for a moment as I began to stutter. Jim just smiled. "Relax, mister; I am your date this evening." I invited him in while I went to pick up my coat. Just like a gentleman, he helped me with it.

We ended up going to the same restaurant my parents liked. It took some time for me to gain enough confidence before I was able to relax. During dinner I finally asked the question, "Why did you not tell me that you were a Naval officer?"

With that killer smile he replied, "You told me that you don't date officers. Remember?" He had me there.

When I finally settled down, we were able to carry on a great conversation. Then Jim brought up my father's last mission. "Do you remember any of the other officers that flew with him?"

"It was such a rush of blood. No, I don't remember any of the faces or names. All I know is that watching my father for the first time was an experience. I suppose you are going to tell me that you were one of his wingmen."

He almost laughed but did not. "Yes. I am glad you did not recognize me when I was waiting in the gate area for the flight to Billings or when I sat in the seat next to you. I saw you checking in and asked the gate agent if I could sit next to you. Luckily the center seat was still open. When company employees were called, I could have ridden in the jump seat, but sitting next to you seemed more likable."

Then I brought up the conversation with my father on Christmas night. "I asked him if he knew a Jim Evanston. All he said was he had flown with you a few times but did not elaborate. He mentioned you were very junior at the base."

"Everything is true that he said about me. The last mission was not the first time I had flown with him as a Navy Reserve pilot. We've done our reserve time together whenever we could but that hasn't been very often lately. When I heard he was pulling his last mission, I wanted to fly with him since we both worked for the same airline and have had many conversations passing the time in the cockpit."

It was time to go to the dance and social at the officers' club on base. I was afraid of what Betsy was going to say when she saw me with a senior officer. He had been out of active duty for three years, putting him a few years older than me. When Jim entered the airline industry, they needed pilots. Minneapolis was his base until he decided to put in a bid for Seattle just for the fun of it. He was surprised a few months later when it came through. They told him that he most likely would be on reserve forever in Seattle if he accepted the bid.

The best part was that he could pull his reserve duty while living in Seattle and make ends meet. While in Minneapolis, he had to fly to Seattle and then drive up to Whidbey. He had never been married and did not have that much time. It was either the reserve, flying for an airline, or helping out at the family ranch back in Montana. He graduated from the University of Montana before entering the service. The new 747/400 was coming online, and he was hoping many of the senior pilots would bid for it since the pay was higher, opening up positions for him.

My heart was going wild as we entered the officers' club. Betsy and her date saw us first and she gave me a big smile. I thought I'd better make the introductions so I quietly nudged Jim over to Betsy and her date. "Sir, I would like you to meet my roommate, Betsy, and her date Kurt."

Betsy was just about to salute when Jim reached over and shook hands with Kurt. He looked over at Betsy and then at me. "Please don't call me sir tonight, and please don't salute me tonight. My first name is Jim. I am Naval Reserve." He explained that he felt embarrassed, especially among friends, and thanked us for honoring his request.

Jim was a good listener. Betsy's date was a local attorney and an ex-Marine she had met through a friend when she first arrived at Whidbey. They seemed to like each other very much, and he did not mind her being a Navy pilot; in fact, he bragged about her life choice. Everybody finally began to converse freely about their lives, professions, and personal likes and dislikes. Finally, Kurt asked how Jim and I met after telling the story about him and Betsy.

I gave Jim a comical look."Let him explain how we met because it is his story."

Both Betsy and her date looked over at Jim. Betsy replied, "I want to hear this one." So for the second time tonight, Jim explained every little detail of the story.

"I flew with her father on a few trips with the airline and liked him, so when I heard he would be completing his last mission, I volunteered to be part of it, even though it was Thanksgiving weekend, and knowing others wanted the time off. When the mission ended, they had a small party for her father, which was the first time I saw her! I immediately fell in love. Unfortunately, before I could get up enough courage to meet her, the whole family left. Then just before Christmas, I saw her waiting in the gate area for the same flight that I was catching. I convinced the gate agent to let me sit next to her, which was the worst seat on the airplane. The rest is history.

When we started talking, she informed me, 'I do not date officers.' So I kept my mouth shut until I picked her up this evening. Then it was too late; she could not turn me down.

"The funny part of it was, although her father knew me from flying together for the same airline and the reserves it never clued her in on the fact that I was a Naval officer." Everyone laughed at the story. It saved me from Betsy egging me on later in the evening. We danced the night away. The more we danced, the more my heart was doing things I had never really felt before.

I looked at him with a smile and commented, "Tomorrow, I will talk with that father of mine."

Jim looked down at me. "Don't forget he outranks you." We all laughed and toasted New Year.

He escorted me to my front door and said goodbye with a soft kiss like no other I had ever experienced before. He was halfway down the sidewalk to his car when I remarked, "Any chance we could do that kiss over one more time for good measure, sir?"

He turned around and came back to plant another long, soft kiss—this time on my mouth. Then back down the sidewalk to his car, yelling back, "I will call you when I get back from my trip to New York. "

I unlocked our door to find Betsy and her date sitting in a couple of chairs. "Well?" Betsy asked me. "We want to hear all the details, mister. He said he fell in love with you the day he first saw you."

"I don't know how to explain it or what I feel. It has been a good night and one I will remember for a long time," I said.

"Well, what did he say after you asked for the second kiss?" Betsy jokingly asked.

"I will call you when I get back from my trip to New York."

"He is really in love with you, so you better watch it." Betsy returned.

The next week started sitting in a classroom, trying to keep my mind on the work. Rain was falling outside, making it even harder. I was thinking, "Best get him out of my mind so I can get on with my life." It was a busy day with simulator flight time in the afternoon, more paperwork, and class afterward. Physical training always happened first thing in the morning, so it helped to put life back in perspective.

I spent a few days a week in the evenings swimming laps. And other times, I would work out in the gym. Betsy and I always seemed to grab dinner at the mess hall in the evening after class. Jim did call once he returned from New York. We promised to exchange our schedules the coming weekend when he was up for his reserve duty, and they were bidding the open reserve slots for the airline.

I finally decided to call my parents and chew my father out for not telling me that Jim was in the Navy and two ranks above me. D.D. informed me he was out on a trip. So it was D.D. who took the heat. "My father left something out when he told me he had flown with Jim a few times," I so smarty made my point.

"Oh, did he leave something out, honey?"

"You know he did," I replied.

"Well, the day we took you to the airport, after you left he did mention something he forgot to tell you."

"Did he tell you what that was, Mother?"

I could hear her little giggle on the other end. "He said he forgot to tell you that Jim was also a Naval officer and a reservist at Whidbey."

"He sure did, and I should be quite upset," I replied.

"Well, outside of being upset with us, I am anxious to hear about this date. Lastly, did you enjoy yourself?" D.D. asked.

"One more question before I tell you about the date. Mother, did my dad tell you that he flew his last Naval mission with Jim as his wingman?"

"That I did not know, love," Dakota said.

"Well he did, volunteering to fly with Dad since they had worked together. Jim saw me at the retirement party, but I left before the man gathered enough courage to introduce himself to me. Then he saw me a few weeks later waiting for the flight to Montana and asked the gate agent if he could have the center seat next to me instead of the jump seat. The rest is history, except he claims to have fallen in love with me at the party."

My stepmother asked, "Do you like him?"

I was trying to be coy. "I do; he is a gentleman, funny, single, great dancer, and even greater kisser."

"Wow! Slow down, young lady—get to know him first! Don't be so anxious. Let him suffer a little bit."

17

A NEW YEAR

It was a start of a weekend, and Jim would be up in the morning to fulfill his reserve duty. He had invited me out to dinner and maybe a little dancing. The knock came early Saturday morning at our door. This time it was me getting out of bed first and answering the door in my pajamas. I forgot the bathrobe. There was Jim, standing in his flight suit, ready for another knock, when the door opened. "You are very sexy in your pajamas, lady," he commended.

"Oh my God," I exclaimed as I returned to my bedroom for the bathrobe.

He walked in with a big smile on his face. "Any chance of a guy getting a cup of Java around this bachelorette apartment?" he asked as he was searching the kitchen. I quickly returned to the kitchen—this time with my bathrobe on and in place. Coffee, a couple of pieces of toast and scrambled eggs were in order as we sat down to a light breakfast. He started filling me in on his next ten days beginning with tomorrow, "I am flying with your father tomorrow."

"Oh my God, you are full of surprises this morning, aren't you?" I answered. "Tell my father I am still upset with him for not filling me in completely about you."

He smiled and asked me, "Are you still upset with him, or are you just being funny?"

"You will never know," I replied.

He left to report for duty a short time later. When he walked out the door, he looked back. "Pick you up for dinner at 1630, mister; could you not be in your pajamas, please." She proceeded to throw a towel as he closed the door behind him. Walking to his car, he kept thinking to himself, "Damn, she is sexy in those pajamas." Today was undoubtedly going to be different than other days he came up to do his duty. But it was going to get better every time from now on.

Life had been good for me the last few weeks. I had not heard from Robert or Mark since Christmas. Mark mentioned the previous time home that he and Robert had gone separate ways in their field, and he hadn't seen much of Robert since Thanksgiving. Before Jim arrived at her door, the mailman had put the mail into our mailbox. Somebody must have been reading my mind earlier. Among the junk mail and bills was a letter from Robert.

Dear Joni,

Hopefully, this finds you still busy and learning how to fly your favorite plane. I don't know how to tell you this since you and I have become terrific friends. When I escorted you to the New Year's Eve Naval ball, I felt like I was accompanying the most beautiful girl there that evening. I must admit I felt good about being with you and happy that you asked me to join you. It was a memorable experience. I also appreciate your brother inviting me into your home and being with your family during the Roundup. Yes, your father worked both Mark and me very hard the week we spent with him. He and your brother taught me quite a bit about the cattle industry in that week. Both of them were also able to get me into the kitchen, making meals for all of us while we were batching it. Your family is very special. Since spending that week with them, I've changed my field of veterinary medicine to small animals instead of large farm animals.

It has taken me quite a few weeks to write this letter to you about our relationship. That day you and your father went on that mission together, I took a long look at our relationship. Your life is entirely different than mine and will continue to be that way for the next several years. Returning home for Christmas, I know I most likely disappointed my parents and probably your parents as well. I believe all of them were hoping for us to get together, but the time is not suitable for either of us. While home, I was able to spend time with a good friend of mine through school. Yes, Joni, she is a girl. We found out that there was more there than we had thought through college.

I am sorry I had to write this in a letter instead of facing you in person. Knowing you and your family has been a privilege for me. Your mother and father and Mark have been good to me the last several months. I want to thank them for everything. Take care, Dear Love. It has been a pleasure and a learning experience to be with you for the last year.

Take Care,
Robert

About the time I had finished the letter, Jim appeared at the door in his flight suit. I let him in. "What is the sour face for?" he asked.

"I just received my first Dear Jane letter," I answered.

"Wow! So I am the one to console the Jane tonight with a dinner that you will never forget," he commented.

"Don't forget you are flying with my father tomorrow," I said.

"I am looking forward to it. The next ten days with the father of the girl I fell in love with at first sight."

"Settle down, sir—you are accompanying a mister to dinner tonight. I may need some crying on your shoulder."

He looked at me, "Tell me all about it over dinner. We'll leave just as soon as I change into some civilian clothes."

He took one look at what I was wearing and gave a wolf whistle.

"You are embarrassing me, sir," I said as I watched him go into the bedroom to change his clothes. "My mother said one time that my dad had a nice butt. I must admit now I know what she means when some men have nice butts," I laughingly mentioned.

Now it was his turn to be embarrassed. "Wait until I see your father tomorrow and tell him he has a nice butt!" he laughingly told me.

"He already knows it being married to my stepmother," I replied.

"Your stepmother is a natural beauty. How did they happen to get together?"

"My mother passed away of cancer when dad was a POW in Vietnam. D.D. just kind of fell into our lives one Saturday afternoon. She and dad belonged to the same college rodeo team. Her comment when I asked her if they ever dated then was that my dad was too busy to chase a barrel racer."

"I am sorry to hear that." He came out of the bedroom looking very sharp in jeans and a white shirt with a sweater over it. "Let us get going to dinner; I am supposed to console a Dear Jane tonight," he said as they left the apartment and walked to his car.

Quietly we drove to our favorite restaurant which we had first visited together on New Year's Eve before the dance at the officers' club. We ordered a fish dinner we both loved. We were initially from Montana and fish seemed to be our favorite meal in Washington

State. The hours passed away as we proceeded to enjoy our meals. I appreciated that Jim was easy-going and so easy to talk to. Shop entered our conversation many times as the evening began to get later.

I picked his brain on some of the training platforms I'd be using before taking the controls myself. He promised to help me through many of them when he some time off. Then he turned to the Dear Jane letter I was concerned about when he had knocked at the door.

I tried to explain some things about Robert, whom I had met on a Thanksgiving dinner invite in Texas. "His family and my parents had been friends in their earlier days. D.D. continued the relationship with his mother afterward since both of them had completed the RCA circuit together.

"We hit it off as soon as we met. My friend Liz hit it off with his brother, John, who is a baseball player with the Baltimore Orioles. Robert had finished college and was working on getting into a university veterinary program. He ended up at WSU in Pullman, WA where he became friends with my brother, Mark. Mark brought him home for a weekend, and my dad put him to work doctoring and shipping cattle.

"I think he figured out it was a lot more work than he thought, working with large animals. So when he returned to Pullman, he changed his field of veterinary to small animals. Anyhow, when he went home for Christmas, he picked up again with someone he called an old friend."

"What are your feelings with this?" Jim asked.

"I guess I am happy for him and thankful that I did not have to write that letter to him," I replied.

He smiled. "You mean you found another guy to replace him already?"

"Don't get too far into yourself, sir. I haven't made up my mind yet."

He again smiled that I got you smile!

Back at the apartment, he escorted me to the door. He stopped there and gave me a big hug and a very long kiss. I did not want it to end, but he did anyway. "Don't forget I am flying with your father tomorrow, and I want to stay on his good side," he mentioned as he turned around and walked to his car.

"I would like to try that kiss again if you please, sir." Once more he turned around, came back and gave me one more kiss and a long hug. This time when he returned to his car he left.

The next morning I wrote back to Robert.

Dear Robert,

I understand your situation. My profession is very intimidating to most individuals, especially a male. However, I've enjoyed my time with you and especially the New Year's Eve dance. You treated me like a real lady, and I thank you for that.

I apologize for my dad putting you to work when you visited us at our ranch. He usually does that with many of our friends when they come for a visit. I don't understand your decision to change fields, but that is your choice. Your family raises quarter horses and good ones, so I guess that is why I am questioning it.

Training is going reasonably well. I am learning a whole new aircraft. It is much different than the ones we flew in Kingston. It has been quite a bit of simulator work, and I don't have Liz here to compete with. Most males compete between themselves. My new roommate, as you know, flies an entirely different aircraft than I do.

Otherwise, I don't have much to tell you except the weather is entirely different from Kingston. It rains almost daily, and sometimes the wind blows off Puget Sound. As a result, we lose power quite often during the winter months. It is harder to fly when the weather is like this, but that is part of our training.

I hope you will be happy with your friend in Texas. I wish you the best. I hear about Dear John letters all the time from the male squadron crew. Now I can brag that I have one.

As Always,
Joni

I was looking at my watch early in the afternoon. It would be about the time my father and Jim would be leaving Seattle for Tokyo, so I stopped at the operations building to see if they had the flight on the base's radar screen.

It turned out better than that. They were able to tune into the U.S. Air Traffic Control and then Canadian Air Traffic Control. I could hear Jim acknowledging their commands. "Goodbye, my dear friend," I whispered to myself. It would be ten days before his return, and I was going to miss him. Now I was left wondering what Jim and my father would be discussing all the time they'd be together. My dad always said that by the time a ten day trip was over, the crew pretty much knew each other quite well.

I could hardly wait until Jim returned. He finally called one afternoon shortly after he returned. Like my father after one of these trips, he would stay home and catch up on some much needed sleep. That same day I was also thinking of my father still having another airplane ride and a drive of 60 miles, likely through a snowstorm and below zero temperatures, before finally being able to call it quits for the day.

Every day was a working day in the Navy, whether you were flying or not. One day you were in class; the next day, you were out watching somebody showing you how to survive a crash landing. Training was really going by spring. Carrier landings and takeoffs became the norm, and getting to know my weapons officer was no longer a challenge; we became good friends on and off base. Jim and I would get together with the weapons officer and his wife a couple of times a month. Jim was spending more time helping me understand many of the terms we used daily.

18

SPRING TIME IN MONTANA

It was April when I completed the final training platform. I received a promotion from ensign to lieutenant at the same time. Jim was there both times and all through the spring. There were rumors about the Middle East among the squadron. Around the base, there were rumblings that a squadron would be assigned to an aircraft carrier in the Persian Gulf. Jim and I decided that we should soon make a trip back to Montana to visit both of our parents, just in case I ended up in the Persian Gulf. Jim's parents hadn't met me, and my mother and brother hadn't met Jim.

It was May and when I called home to let them know that we were coming home together. My mother informed me they would be moving the cattle to the summer pasture the day after we arrived. In the back of my mind, I was smiling, as my dad was again getting the much-needed extra help from a boyfriend. Unfortunately, Mark was doing an internship with a veterinarian in Oregon so he would not make it this time.

Before we left, I warned Jim about what was going to happen when we finally arrived. With a smirk on his face, he said, "I already knew that was going to happen. I saw your father in operations yesterday. When he told me, I threw up my hands and just walked away. Honey, your father and I have a lot more time together than you and I do. Remember, we sit three feet apart for 10-11 hours at a time just watching instruments, which is boring. So we have to talk to each other once in a while—communication in the cockpit is key to a safe flight."

I drove down from Whidbey Island to his place in Everett early, arriving just as the sun was rising over the Cascades. I had never been in his home before and was impressed with his taste. He even had a garden and did some canning of vegetables. I could tell he was a runner since there were trophies of different marathons he had participated in over the years.

I noticed a 4H picture of his winning steer in a local fair and a few photos of him with different girls he had dated throughout the years. I meant to ask about them, but he came out of the bedroom in a pair of jeans and a short sleeve t-shirt looking sexy as usual. Pulled along behind him was his roller flight bag, this time with clothes for the Montana trip.

"I told my mother that we would call her when we got close, so they could either hold dinner for us or go ahead and have it themselves," I commented as we put our bags in his trunk.

The miles started to roll beneath us as we crossed the Cascade Mountains and the prairies of Washington State. It was mid-afternoon when we stopped in Missoula for a fuel stop, and called home to let my parents know we should be home by early evening. We talked along the way about various subjects, including the latest rumors going around the base. Jim had spoken with one of his friends who was a commander for the reserve. It looked like a couple of reserve squadrons would be going to the Gulf. One Navy aircraft carrier would be leaving near the end of July.

When we finally pulled into the ranch, it was still early evening. My father and D.D. came out to meet us. My father asked how our trip was.

Everybody laughed as I commented on our day, "Well, I finally was able to spend 12 hours with Jim as my father does." I had traveled more by car between Seattle and home in the last eight months than I had in all of my 24 years.

Dinner was always conversation time in our home. That evening we discussed many things, including tomorrow morning's cattle drive to summer pasture, my completion of Prowler training, my mother's new book being made into a movie, and finally, Jim and I flying together on an overnight training mission.

My father commented that his wife has made more money than he has in the last couple of years. "I just might be able to retire and let her bring the money into the household." my father kidded.

Finally, D.D. stated, "You mean you might stay home, so we can stay in bed all day making love?" We all laughed at that statement.

Then, Jim inserted, "Joni told me you were the coolest stepmother anyone could have."

D.D. just smiled and said, "You haven't seen anything yet."

The evening ended with everyone around the fireplace sipping a favorite beverage and having a light conversation. There was some shop talk about the possibility of being deployed to the Middle East. My father would start training on the 747/400 early in the fall. Unfortunately, it meant flying out of New York instead of Seattle, making commuting much harder. Jim would move up to captain on the 747/200 in Seattle after training in Minneapolis.

Morning came early as the sun started to rise over the plateau. It was all family this morning except Jim, who seemed to be enjoying himself. Nick and his wife, Jamie, would provide lunch. My dad hired them while I was in Kingston and they were living in the remodeled home. He was pretty happy with both of them, and they handled the ranch duties quite well. It had been seven years since I had been part of this family day. To all of our surprise, Jim was quite good on a horse and working cattle. Easy going with a lovely butt in a saddle on a good horse. The day was incredible; the scenery was even better. The Sawtooth Ridge laid out ahead of us this morning—it was always in my dreams when I was away from this part of heaven.

The cattle drive completed, all of us crowed into the homeward bound pickup as it made its way down an old gravel road. Jim and I decided to ride in the back, crouched in the box of the pickup. With his arm around me as I cuddled up to him, I'm sure he could feel my breathing and my heart beating almost too fast. The dust from the pickup and the horse trailer hung in the air as we made our way home.

Everyone was tired. Jim and I were planning on getting an early start in the morning. The next stop was Jim's parents' ranch near Roundup, Montana. My father invited us to take the airplane over, making the trip 30 minutes instead of 2 hours. Both of us gave a thankful look to him, and thanked him for the offer. Jim asked, "What kind of airplane do you have, and do we know how to fly it?"

My father looked at both of us. "It is a Cessna 310; both of you better know how to fly it." We laughed and thanked him again.

Jim and I left the following day, taking off from the ranch's airstrip and turning left into the early sunrise. My parents watched as we disappeared over the horizon.

Jim would land at a small local airport for the first time since he had learned to fly there. So many great memories from his teenage years were now returning. His instructor had been surprised when he had been accepted into the Navy flight program years later after completing college.

In a very short time, he tuned to the aircraft frequency at the airport and requested the weather and landing instructions.

A familiar voice answered the radio, "I will be goddamn! Is that you, Jim?"

"Yes, it is me, Bart. You better watch that language, old man," Jim replied to the airport operator.

"Your parents are just driving in." He then gave Jim the latest in weather and winds with landing and taxi instructions. "It will be nice having you home for a while. I heard that you are bringing the love of your life with you."

My face turned beet red at the comment. Jim looked at me and delivered an order: "Better wipe that embarrassed look off of your face, mister. You will have plenty more before the day is over." After that, we shared the flying; I let him do most of it since he knew where he was going. He taxied the plane over to the hangar where he was directed after we landed. Bart, the airport manager met us, with Jim's parents watching from the sidelines.

We exited the aircraft from our respective sides. I grabbed the chucks and placed them on the wheels. Bart informed us that he would be putting the aircraft into the hangar. I looked around, and Jim already had our bags in hand and was walking towards his parents. They met in the center of the runway, and had an enormous hug for him. I slowly made my way towards the group, and they met me with a big hug. Jim then introduced me to his father Ron and his mother Bess. His father stood back after hugging me. "My son informed us at Christmas that he had met the love of his life. However, we did not believe him until now."

It took about half an hour to reach their ranch in the hills surrounding Roundup. Like the Rockies, the mountains we drove through were all green from the fresh spring rains. Being back in Montana was an eye-opening experience after the last couple of years in the Texas countryside. It also was much different than the Pacific Northwest with the seemingly never-ending rain. Today it looked like the day would be a pleasant one while meeting Jim's family for the first time. His father was just like him in many ways. Always a joke ready for the right time and a kind word for everyone. His mother had a lovely personality and was a high school English teacher.

When we entered the ranch's home place, it was impressive and looked across the hills. We had lunch before all relaxing on the large front porch with some iced tea. Everyone just wanted to get acquainted with each other. About mid-afternoon, Jim mentioned that he and I should go for a horseback ride and see the surrounding property. Just before we were ready to start, Jim asked, "You brought your fly rod, didn't you? Remember when I told you we could go fishing if you wanted to?"

I ran back into the house and dug the fly rod and flies out of my duffle bag. "Ok! I am ready now," I said as I came running across the yard to where Jim was waiting with our horses.

We had covered just a few miles when a lake appeared over the horizon. Arriving by the lake, we found a place to tie the horses up and let them graze on the lush grass alongside the shore. I took off my boots and waded into the cool lake flipping the fly across the top of the water. Jim finally had his fly pole out and had also pulled off his boots. Suddenly, a beautiful rainbow trout jumped out of the water with my hook firmly in its mouth. "Got one!" I exclaimed as I expertly led it towards my net.

Jim could not believe his eyes as I played with the trout, netted it and removed the fly.

"Who taught you to fly fish, mister?"

"My dad," I replied as I threw the fly into the water again. "You remember the creek out in our yard while you were there? It has some very nice trout in it. You ought to give it a try when we get back to my home."

He just stood there in the water, working his fly and watching the girl he had fallen in love with the first time he had seen her.

I had caught four more fish and decided to stop and sit on a boulder and watch my man. Laughing, I commented, "You know, you do have a very nice butt if I may say so!"

"You are funny, mister." Jim, for the first time, was otherwise lost for words. He knew I was teasing him, and the more I did, the more he loved me.

I had my fish cleaned and already packed in the saddlebags. "I suppose you are going to pull rank on me and make me clean your fish too," I teased, giving him that smile he had said he had fallen in love with seven months ago.

"Let's go home. I suppose it is getting close to dinner time," he said as he climbed on his horse and pointed it towards the ranch. I easily kept up with him, wondering what my father and Eve felt when they fell in love. They loved the same things, and I could remember some of the great times my mother and father made for themselves.

I remembered a story that my mother used to tell me when I was little. It was about the large trout she caught while fishing with my father, and how she always out fished him. My father had taught me well, and he used to tell the same story as I got older.

"Come on, mister. What are you doing? Daydreaming about me, I hope," Jim commented as he motioned me to catch up.

Dinner was excellent, with more than a person could eat. His mother was a good cook, and she must have been a good teacher because Jim talked about her being his guardian angel at school.

Jim and his father were like two peas in a pod. They joked and enjoyed telling the stories that made up their lives. Dinner completed, we moved to the large front porch. Our home had no front porch like this one. Jim started filling his parents in on his past year, and the possibility of working into being the commander of his squad. He loved his job with the airline and traveling almost monthly to far-off places. Flying the whale with his junior seniority was a benefit; he took the job with a great deal of pride. His parents asked why he didn't fly out of Minneapolis instead of Seattle, where he could hold captain status on domestic flights. Jim's comment was that there was no Navy base near the Twin Cities, like near Seattle where he could do both.

The conversation turned to me and my family. Both Ron and Bess knew about my father from the newspaper articles the past 4 years while he was a POW.

Bess then asked about my birth mother. I slowly started to put the history together. "My mother, Eve, was a flight attendant for the same airline as my father. She had to resign after they were married. She passed away just before Christmas. My father returned in February from Vietnam. My brother Mark and I hardly knew him since he was recalled to active duty when I was four and my brother was 2. Before my mother passed away, she left a notebook, mostly about the history of our parents' love for each other. When we moved to Montana, we kept finding little notes from her in our belongings."

I looked over at Jim and let him know about my daydreaming on the return horseback ride this afternoon. "Jim, I was dreaming about my mother and dad's relationship before they were married. She wrote in that memo of hers the reason she fell in love with him. The biggest one was that they had a lot of fun together. He respected her all through their courting, as she called it. It was old fashioned, and he always encouraged her to make her own path. When my father was re-activated, with the help of her parents she started taking flying lessons until cancer came along."

"All through the ride after I caught more fish than you, I kept thinking about our relationship and how it has matured since you claimed to fall in love with me back in December."

He and his parents smiled at me and his mother commented, "Thank you, Joni, for telling the beautiful story about your mother."

Then Jim continued, "Her stepmother isn't bad either. I can see a lot of her personality in Joni.

19

LISTENING TO NATURE

Jim and I continued to sit on the porch after his parents left. We just sat there quietly, listening to nature. Finally, after a long silence between us, Jim spoke up, "This doesn't get this quiet from where we come from these days."

I replied, "I know what you mean. My life the last few years has been full of noise. I love quiet; my father always returns to that cottonwood stump by the creek. He quietly sits there and lets nature talk to him. You know, Jim, it works. I've seen him go down there often to think. I've done it myself several times."

D.D. told me they spent hours down there one evening after he had purchased the ranch from his family. She had come out to interview him for an article and ended up trailing cattle to summer pasture. That evening D.D. stayed over, sleeping in her horse trailer. Just before she turned in, she saw a fire down by the creek. It was my father sleeping down there as he had been ever since returning to the ranch. She joined him on the stump and together they talked into the night. It wasn't an interview for a big story; it was about themselves, their dreams, passions and trials. Sometimes I do the same; the best medicine for the soul, heart and mind is listening to nature.

We finally retired for the evening. I heard voices and pans in the kitchen banging against each other early the following day. I took a quick shower and made my way to the kitchen where I could smell trout cooking as I entered. Jim's mother was there working and singing away. "Good morning, young lady," she smiled, "the men are outside doing the chores. Jim's father is teaching him how to milk cows again." Both of us laughed. "Would you like to set the table and have a cup of coffee?" his mother asked. I thanked her and went searching for the dishes to set. The cup of coffee was a welcome change from the chilly morning.

While setting the table, Jim's mother asked, "I'm just wondering, being female, why did you decide on the Navy and being a pilot?"

"Well, my father was a pilot, and from a young age, he taught both my brother and me how to fly."

"Then why did you decide on attending the Naval Academy?"

I answered, "It created a challenge for me, and I like a challenge. Besides, women were starting to be accepted, which I felt might create an even more significant challenge. I like the structure of military life. It gives you a more direct path to your goals than a civilian college does with all of its social life."

"Yes, Jim had a problem with the social life at the university. He finally settled down in his second year and set his sights on a goal. We believe it was the ROTC program at the university that set a structure for him. Seven years on active duty, and then when the airlines came searching for pilots at the base, he readily applied and has enjoyed the reserve and working for the airline ever since. His life has changed over the years. We thought he might end up marrying a flight attendant or someone his sisters knew. But instead, it was a surprise when he came home for Christmas and let us know he had found the love of his life." We both laughed at her last remark. "Please don't rush it," she recommended.

I replied, "I owe my life for the next six years to the Navy, so I am in no hurry. The worst part of my training is behind me, but my father cautions that the worst might be ahead."

"Your father had experience in that life afterward; learn from his experience. My husband and I like you. You are the first girl Jim has ever brought home to introduce to us." I thanked her for the advice and the compliment.

Jim's father suggested we ride out to the summer range and check out the cattle. Unlike my family, his family branded before moving the cattle to the summer range. Their family belonged to a grazing association with several other ranchers. So together, with a lunch made for them, we rode out to check on the cattle.

Both of them had been riding horses and working cattle since grade school. Jim had discovered that my parents had a couple watching the cattle throughout the summer and into fall. He also knew that my parents lived closer to the Bob Marshall Wilderness area where bears, wolves and cougars roamed. While with my father, Jim had asked if they ever had problems, especially when the calves were younger. My father had acknowledged that they did.

We found a small stream to have lunch beside after reaching the pasture. It was quiet and peaceful. Shortly after relaxing on a grassy knoll, Jim asked, "What do you think about my parents?"

I smiled and answered, "I love them; they are good, hard-working people. I can see they love all of their children very much. Your mother has some sound advice that she offered me."

"What was that?" he asked.

"None of your business. It was women's talk. I don't ask you about your conversations with my father, and you two have spent quite a bit of time together in that cockpit." He sat back on the grass and just laughed.

We spent the next few hours checking the cattle and making sure everything was all right. Fences seemed well taken care of, and the cattle were being moved to different areas to keep the grass growing through the summer. Then finally at mid-afternoon, we began our journey home. Jim had decided we would return another way that he knew from his earlier days. We transverse a hill that looked across the whole valley and the ranch. It was beautiful as the sun was beginning to set, turning the sky into all sorts of brilliant colors.

Jim's father met us at the barn and informed us dinner would be ready shortly so don't waste our time. His mother was an excellent cook, as I found out most farmers' wives were. I helped his mother clean up the dishes afterward. While in a general conversation, I mentioned it would be nice to have some of her recipes later. With no surprise, his mother reached into a drawer and brought out a notebook with all her recipes. "I've been waiting for some nice girl to give this to, and you are that girl." She handed the notebook to me.

"Wow!" I took the notebook and gave her a big hug.

The following day after breakfast, Jim's parents took us back to the local airport. His father commented as we traveled over the gravel road, "This will be the first time I've taken you to the local airport instead of driving to Billings." Everyone laughed as we entered the airport gate and stopped at the office to get the keys and pay the fuel bill. Then the manager helped us open the hangar door and pull the aircraft out into the sunlight. Jim's parents watched as we pre-checked the plane and loaded our bags and fishing poles into the baggage compartment.

Less than half an hour later, with some big hugs and "Love you," we taxied the aircraft to the beginning of the runway for our run-up. Slowly, the plane picked up speed, raced down the runway, lifted into the air and disappeared into the late morning sun. Then we made a sharp right-hand turn and one more low pass over the airport, dipping our wing a couple of times.

Jim's parents felt lonely for the first time in days. They loved their son and loved this girl that has taken his heart.

Less than an hour later, we could view the Eastern Front of the Rockies. It was noon when we landed at my home. Both of my parents came out to welcome us back. Jim's mother had called ahead to let them know that we had departed. The noontime meal was ready for us. We sat down with the radio on and Paul Harvey giving the news of the day. Local news and livestock reports followed. It felt like both of us had just stepped into the past from our busy lives.

My father had been up on the plateau seeding spring wheat with the help of Nick. He asked if Nick would return and finish the job so he could spend more time with his daughter. Nick's wife offered to help her husband complete the project.

Late in the afternoon we all went down to the creek where the old cottonwood stump still stood. A bit weatherworn from many years of life, it had withstood winds, rains, snowstorms and floods over the years.

We brought some warm sandwiches and drinks along. My father had known Jim from when Jim started flying in the right seat of the whale—the same chair my father had started in after returning from Vietnam.

Jim and I filled my parents in on our visit to his parents. I bragged about my fly fishing, how I was able to catch more fish than him, and how well his mother cooked those fish for breakfast the following day. Jim started laughing and was ready to do something he might regret later. I looked at him and said, "What was that?"

"Throw you into the water since you decided to make a fool out of me." We all laughed at that remark.

My dad looked at him and replied, "Jim, you better learn that both of these women will make fools of us guys." Gesturing to D.D. he said, "Just let them because you will never regret it." Everyone laughed.

20

RUMORS OF WAR

Then the conversation became serious about the latest news. There was a rumor on the news wires that the United States would order a fleet to the Gulf. In addition, there were movements in the Middle East that looked like maybe war was brewing. Both Jim and I heard the rumblings among Whidbey personnel and had decided to take this vacation as soon as possible. We both knew that it might be quite a while before we would return to Montana.

Later on that same stump, Jim and I had a heart-to-heart discussion about marriage. He loved me, and I loved him, but I had experienced the effects of war on my own family. My father still carries the carnage of a war. I still believed the stress of the unknown caused my mother's cancer. She took up flying so she could provide for the family if need be. The daily news and continuous pain took their toll. Once in a while, I look at that notebook D.D. made for me with all my mother's notes. Even though D.D. has been a great mother, I still miss my mother Eve and wish she was here. I also feel my father will always miss her too. His comment years ago when I started at Annapolis was, "Your first love will always be the most memorable, so savor the moment."

"You're right about your father and our long conversations on our cockpit duty time. You can learn a lot about a person when you spend twelve hours with him. When he decided to retire on Thanksgiving weekend, I knew I had to be his wingman, so I volunteered. Since it was a holiday weekend, it wasn't hard to get that opportunity. I never dreamed in a million years that I would meet the girl of my dreams on that flight.

"You know the rest of the story. I do understand the situation. When you return, I will be waiting for you. I patiently waited for the right girl to come along, and now that I've found her, I need the patience to wait for just a bit longer. Our lives are built around patience these days," Jim concluded.

The following day, we departed the ranch for the West Coast just as the sun rose over the plateau. Deep in our minds was the thought that we might not see it again. As he was driving, Jim commented, "We will be back here to get married, so don't fret." I smiled at his positive attitude on life. He was so like his parents who had their ups and downs throughout life but managed to keep it together and raise three children.

My parents were the same. My mother waited 16 years and went through hell for the love of her life. My dad had been through hell and back. Now, outside of some bad dreams, he seemed to be making a life for his family here in The Shadows of Sawtooth Ridge. I remember him saying he owed it to D.D. and that cottonwood stump down by the creek for his sanity. Now it looked like it would be my turn to use that cottonwood stump if I could return.

21

WAR

We returned to Jim's home first in the early afternoon. I decided to continue on to Whidbey. Leaving his home was problematic since we had spent a whole week together visiting our families. Looking back on the times I had departed home, first for the academy and then again for Naval flight training, I realized it was getting more difficult each time. Finally, I was beginning to understand why my father kept returning to his roots.

When I reached our apartment. Betsy was home, and anxious to hear about my leave. We sat up until late into the evening, gossiping about what had happened since I had left for Montana. Betsy had something to brag about also. Greg had just asked her to marry him after a year's dating. She was excited, but worried after she said yes due to the rumors going around the base about her squadron possibly going to the Middle East.

The following day I reported to my squadron commander that I had returned. He asked me how I enjoyed going home and having some time with the family. I bragged about catching more fish than Jim. "I had to teach him that sometimes women can do better than men."

He laughed, knowing who she was dating. "It will teach Jim how to be humble." Then he smiled and told me to report to the classroom section for duty. I saluted, turned, and walked out the door. I was thinking to myself about more classroom time. It was a never-ending learning experience, whether it was flying or in the classroom. Other times it was just simulator time, which fortunately I enjoyed. Betsy was going out on a mission this morning, flying down the coast to Mexico and back.

It was August 2 when everyone woke up to the news that Iraq had begun invading Kuwait. Betsy's crew had just managed to take down one of the most significant drug running operations in the history of the Navy. She was proud of their accomplishment and showed it. She called the command center; they informed her that the operation would continue for the foreseeable future. Their commander felt it was a great training exercise just in case their mission would change. However, as a result of the Iraqi invasion, the Navy canceled all leaves and those on leave were to return to base as soon as possible.

September arrived, and Betsy's squadron already had left for Riyadh, Saudi Arabia. Their orders were to conduct coastal surveillance along Iraq and Kuwait to provide pre-strike reconnaissance.

I started calling home more often in case I would be next to ship out. My father, having already bid several MAC trips from various US locations to Frankfurt and on to Riyadh, Saudi Arabia was committed for the foreseeable future. (MAC better known as Military Air Command using civilian aircraft to move troops from one area to the next.) The company had requested a particular group of pilots having a certain number of hours in the aircraft to fly these routes. Therefore Mark was going to make his way home the last of October to cover for our father if he was away.

Jim had bid and received a reserve captain's position in Seattle. As a result, his assignments were very irregular. Nevertheless, we managed to have a few dinner dates. Each of our lives were changing by the day.

I had no more than hung up the phone one evening after talking with my parents when the doorbell rang. It was Jim in a full flight suit carrying his duffle bag. "I am now on active duty, mister," he stated before I could ask. I did not know whether to cry or hug him as he entered the apartment. "Any chance I can use Betsy's bedroom? I promise to be good." I looked at him and just smiled. He took me out to dinner at our favorite restaurant and we made a short night of it.

The following day I reported to my duty station and Jim reported to his reserve commander. He became the group leader of one reserve squadron, all of them experienced aviators who had had various assignments over the years while in their regular units. Many had spent time with the Seventh Fleet in the Pacific and some had been in the Persian Gulf on different assignments.

They would spend the next few weeks brushing up on their skills while waiting to be shipped out to the Middle East. Their crew would be going with them to the ship. After that, Jim moved back to the VF-14 so he and some of his squadrons spent the time relearning the skills they had before entering the reserve as Prowler pilots. While serving in the reserves these recalled pilots flew Prowlers. Now recalled to active duty. These same pilots would now fly VF-14.

There was a lot of movement around the base as the news started to trickle through the ranks. Jim moved into BOQ to be closer to his squadron. Betsy and I decided to keep the apartment, but I moved into my squadron BOQ (Bachelor Officer Quarters) for the same reason. Then came the disappointing news. Females were not allowed in the combat zone. The only females flying in or near those zones were supply pilots, helicopter pilots, refueling pilots, and pilots flying the P-3C. Betsy was assigned lead on a P-3C. The aircraft was one of the first to arrive in the Middle East after the invasion of Kuwait. It is credited with destroying 11 vessels within hours of the start of the Dessert Storm air campaign.

I called home to let them know I was not going to the Middle East after all. D.D. answered the phone and listened to my disappointment. Finally, a quiet voice informed me there is always a reason and to be patient; my time would come.

D.D. then mentioned that having one person in the Middle East was enough for now. My father was moving troops from different Army and Marine posts on the East Coast. My mother also said that the calves were shipped and the cattle finally brought home. Nick was getting the wheat out of the grain storage bins. The daily semis were making their way out of the ranch. Finally, Mark and Judy made it home to help Nick and Jamie. The five of them managed to get the cattle work completed without me or my father. My father was now commuting to Minneapolis to begin his flying. He was hoping to make it home for Thanksgiving but wasn't sure of anything at this point. He would call almost on a nightly basis and let D.D. know where he was. The last call was from Frankfurt, and he was going to and returning from Saudi Arabia the same day. I thought to myself as I hung up the phone, "My father is retaking the lead even though he is not even in the military anymore."

The next day I mentioned to Jim that my father was already moving troops into the Middle East. It sounded like he and a few other seasoned pilots were doing shuttle service between Frankfurt and the Middle East. It did not surprise Jim too much that my father was doing it.

After Iraq attacked Kuwait last summer, Joni's father and a few other pilots went back to the Twin Cities for simulator training.

Jim and his small squadron of reservists received their orders to fly to the Red Sea, where they would meet up with the rest of their squadron. In addition, another squadron from the Caribbean would be meeting up with them. It would be an east coast meet up. They would then proceed to the Red Sea, where they would join the USS John F. Kennedy. Other than the support personnel leaving the base, there would be no more squadrons presently departing.

I learned that Liz was already in the Gulf flying a supply aircraft to the various carriers. When I talked to Liz's parents, I could tell they were worried about her, but both being military, they knew the profession's dangers. Then there was Betsy who had been there since August, just two weeks after Iraq invaded Kuwait. I learned from Betsy's fiancée that she was flying out of a Saudi airbase. He said her squadron had been flying very long hours. Since he was a former Marine and had seen plenty of action in the Middle East, he was worried for Betsy, and so were her parents.

One evening in the mess hall, I was finally reading one of D.D.'s books. Even though she was my mother, until recently I somehow hadn't gotten around to reading any of them. One of the officers in my quarters had managed to purchase her latest book. She was a fan of Dakota, and had read all of her books and watched one of the movie versions. While in conversation with her, I made what I thought was a mistake, letting her know that I was Dakota's daughter. It was a conversation that led to many more conversations over the next few weeks. So for the first time, I felt that I had better read at least one of her books.

When I finally started reading the book. I became so immersed into the story that I almost forgot about a dinner date with that officer.

The officer who was a fan of Dakota commented at dinner, "Did you finally figure out that your mother is an excellent author?"

I replied, "I didn't have time until now. I guess now that I am also a fan of my mother and have a little time on my hands, I might as well enjoy what you ladies have enjoyed all this time."

I was starting to feel a bit lonely without Jim or Betsy around part of the time. By now, both should be somewhere in the Middle East; Jim stationed in the Red Sea on the aircraft carrier USS John F. Kennedy, and Betsy in Saudi Arabia.

It was Betsy who had tried to convince me to try an aircraft other than the Intruder. Betsy always seemed to be flying somewhere on a mission. It was either up and down the Pacific Coast or in the Caribbean chasing drug traffickers. Now she and her crew were in the Middle East keeping track of Iraqi troop movements. Most of my flights were training flights in and around Washington State.

It was a long weekend as I settled down with D.D.'s book. I stopped by the officers' mess for dinner which wasn't too exciting. Most were in conversations about the happenings in the Middle East. It looked like Iraq was staying in Kuwait permanently. I went over to the operations center to see what exciting news they might have. The officer who was in charge of the center seemed a bit bored, and was glad someone stopped by to pass the time away and keep him company.

Our conversation turned to the different Whidbey squadrons that were in the Middle East. He mentioned that the P-3C's had a pilot shortage and most of the aircraft had been flying 21 hours a day. Some of them had been flying with only two instead of the usual three pilots.

That wasn't a problem when they had been back here doing drug enforcement, but it was a problem over there.

I was set up for a training exercise Monday morning. Before I was to report, my commanding officer requested to have a conversation with me. I entered his office and informed the secretary that I was there. The officer met me at the door. He then requested that I be seated in the chair in front of his desk. "You are Betsy's roommate, aren't you?"

I replied, "Yes, sir."

"She asked me to talk with you about assuming a pilot's position on the P-3C. Her commanding officer is begging for more pilots. Betsy thought you might be interested in the chance."

I looked at him with surprise. "I've only been in the aircraft once, and I'm not checked out in it."

"Joni, you are a great pilot, and if you are all right with it, we could get you into the simulator as soon as possible. I believe we could have you flying in a couple of weeks. It took me two weeks to learn it when the squadron had just transferred here. I will give you one day to think about it."

I left his office, amazed that on Saturday evening I had learned they were shorthanded, and Monday morning I was in the commanding officer's office with him inquiring if I was interested in helping out. It took two blocks before I turned around and made a beeline back to his office. Deep in my mind, it made me mad. My father, Liz, Jim, and Betsy were all in the Middle East. It was the last of October and I was sitting at home away from the battle. Yes, feeling sorry for myself because women were not allowed into combat. Yet deep down, I knew I was ready and nothing was going to stop me.

Since no one else was training for the position, I could get with the trainer that afternoon. We worked together until dinner and then took a much-needed break. After another 3 hours we both called it a day. It was the hardest I had studied since flight training in Texas. This aircraft was different, with four jet prop engines instead of two jets. Much slower than the fighter jet, but larger. I spent my weekend just sitting in the simulator, memorizing the checklist over and over again. Finally, one night I woke from a dream I was having about flying the aircraft. I was so excited that I did not even take the weekend off.

It was the second week when two other pilots, the trainer and I took the controls of the only P-3C left on base. All 3 of us pulled a pre-check and all three of us together filed a flight plan with operations center. We were going to fly north to Alaska and pull an in-flight refueling exercise before returning to Whidbey. Today there would be three pilots, three enlisted sensor operators, and of course, one trainer. I would be the number 2 pilot occupying the right seat. The trainer felt being part of the flight crew would give me a better chance of qualifying as soon as possible for my new assignment in the Middle East. All three pilots would be shipping out together as soon as I was ready. This training session would be the first of three for us together. The entire crew, except the trainer, was due for assignment in the Middle East. The only person holding up the appointment was me and I was working as hard as possible

22

DESERT STORM ASSIGNMENT

When we completed the third training flight, our commander was waiting with our orders. Our destination was Bahrain. We would leave in 3 days, giving us a couple of days to put our affairs in order. I thought, "Jim, Liz, and Betsy, here I come. Thank you, Betsy, for the enlightening suggestion you gave your commander."

I felt it was about time I should call home before leaving for Riyadh, Saudi Arabia. My mother answered the phone and I asked if my father could pick up the other phone. I then proceeded to fill them in on the happenings of the last two weeks. I was now a pilot on the P-3C and had been training the last couple of weeks. My training group would be leaving in a couple of days for Saudi Arabia. It was going to be a different Thanksgiving for them this year, with only Mark being home. I could tell that they were not only disappointed, but worried for their daughter. I tried to assure them that we would not be flying in a combat zone, but instead would be tracking all the non-military traffic flying in and out of the area.

It was going to be the last conversation with my family for a long time in the Shadows of Sawtooth Ridge. A Navy van would take us to McCord Air Force base near Tacoma, where we would catch a military flight that would eventually take us to Ramstein, Germany. There we would transfer to another flight for Riyadh. I had flown first class so many times on my father's airline passes and seniority that I had no idea how ordinary people traveled.

The first stop was Baltimore, where we would change flights. I spent more than 5 hours of flying time cramped up in a center seat with a male seat mate who would not stop talking. He was a retired lieutenant colonel who had just divorced his wife. Every time I would try and get some rest, he would interrupt me. Finally, while waiting for my transfer in Baltimore, two other Navy officers and I made a decision to find seats together. Somehow the Colonel found his way into the last seat in our row. One of the other Navy officers gave me a wedding band he accidentally had in his pocket. I slipped it on while in the bathroom and returned to my seat. I was flashing my left hand a little bit so the colonel would see the ring on my finger. Amazing how quiet he had become.

Landing in Ramstein, we could see a Navy aircraft sitting next to our parking space at the terminal. The three of us made our way to the baggage claim where a Navy officer was waiting for us. While waiting for our bags, another Navy officer walked up behind me. "It is about time you arrived!" I turned around to see Liz standing there smiling in her flight suit. One big hug and smiles all around. Liz and I led our group out onto the tarmac, where the aircraft was waiting. The three of us managed to find seats among the cargo that was on board while Liz continued on to the cockpit. It was cargo bound for different aircraft carriers. We were going to make a stop at one aircraft carrier in the Mediterranean.

The landing was almost perfect, and the stop was only 30 minutes before being shot off the deck into the air again. The next stop was

Dammon, Saudi Arabia. I was able to sit up in the cockpit in one of the jump seats. Liz seemed to be enjoying herself.

Liz and I were able to catch up on some gossip. Liz had heard Robert and I had decided to go our separate ways. Just before Liz left on this mission, John had asked her to marry him. She must have said, "Yes," because she was wearing a beautiful engagement ring. John seemed to be all right with her being absent so much. His reasoning behind their relationship was that he had 162 games every year, and half of them would be away games. So what time they could be together for the next few years would be worth it.

It was a smooth landing at the vast Riyadh Air Base. The two other officers and I reported to the American Base Operations Commander's office. After a meal in the officers' mess hall, the three of us participated in a familiarization tour and learned key customs of the host country. We would learn our assignments in a couple of days; until then, it was our responsibility to learn the workings of our respective areas and sit in on briefings about every 8 hours.

I was finally assigned a mission on the second day. My report time and briefing were at 0800 on the third morning. I reported to the briefing room 15 minutes early after breakfast. Standing there in the front of the room was Betsy—not only my roommate back at Whidbey, but now my leader for the remainder of my assignment. I assumed the number 3 pilot position on this mission since I was new and needed time to work with the crew.

I had butterflies in my stomach as the crew became familiar with each other. There would finally be a crew of ten on these missions instead of the nine. I could tell the excitement in Betsy's feelings when we met. I was not only a roommate, but also a welcome and fresh member to complete her overworked crew. Two hours later after an extensive pre-check, we were in the air flying at some 35000 feet. It would be a 16 hour mission with two in-air refueling points along the way.

Along with the plane flight plan, the enlisted crew members working the radar and doing other duties onboard kept reporting all of their findings to the Navigator/Communicator and Tactical Coordinator. It wasn't only military movements but civilian movements also. I started replacing the other two pilots every four hours. I went back through the cabin and was amazed at all the action happening along the route. Military vehicles were moving through Iraq into Kuwait. The enlisted personnel could tell you the size and what they were hauling. They had satellite images that gave them other intelligence information. The information gathered was relayed back to the United States, where Intel people assembled it and made decisions on more significant happenings.

Shutting down the two outside props was something that I had never experienced. It saved fuel; with the lighter air, they just freely turned. I kept thinking of my father when I assumed control of the mission. Betsy mentioned to me, "Not as fast as your Prowler, but you are now part of the war. You may not feel that it is exciting, but it can be at times. I would feel better chasing drug boats and airplanes than chasing armies." I did not have enough experience with either one to comment.

Every two days, it was another 16 to 20 hour day. Thanksgiving dinner in the mess was a day late for the crew and was celebrated half a world away by our families. It was just another day flying along borders in the Middle East. Iraq still wasn't moving, and it looked like they were building up their defenses for what they felt was coming. Iraq date to leave Kuwait was January 15th. Everyone, including me, had an idea what was going to happen, but many feared at the same time. A few enlisted personnel who had been in Vietnam felt this war would be different. I had made friends with a few who flew with our crew and listened to them closely. However, it would be the last assignment for the enlisted men who flew with Betsy as their pilot commander. The entire crew, with all the ground crew, had been together since they transferred from Guam to Whidbey and now the Middle East.

All of us, including the ground crew, spent most of our off time together. We ate together and basically lived together. Betsy required daily briefing with the entire team. She was an excellent leader and I was happy to be learning from her. We all took our jobs seriously and made sure it all ran like clockwork. For example, we which had a new prototype system onboard known as Outlaw Hunter which was being tested in the Pacific when Iraq invaded Kuwait. An Inverse Synthetic Aperture Radar (APS-137) was also on this particular aircraft. These systems allowed us to conduct coastal surveillance along the coasts of Iraq and Kuwait and provide pre-strike reconnaissance on enemy military installations.

It was 10 minutes after midnight on January 16 while we were flying our regular route that all hell broke loose. The enlisted personnel in the back knew it was coming and could see it from their vantage point. Our airplane would shake every time a nearby explosion took place. It was continuous, 24 hours a day, seven days a week. The aerial campaign was the prelude to the invasion of Kuwait and Iraq. These were targets that someone back in the United States had pointed out as high-value targets. There would be no sleep for the crew during the next few weeks. We all had butterflies, but it was all business as each of us carried out our assigned duties.

It was three weeks into the continuous air campaign when I saw a commercial 747 from my father's company unloading cargo and passengers on the tarmac. While we at the same time was doing our aircraft pre-check. Since I had seen similar aircraft before, I thought nothing of it. Betsy, Nancy our number two pilot, and I walked into operations to pick up the paperwork for our next mission. We became so involved with the paperwork that we never noticed who else was in the room. A voice from on the other side of the room finally spoke up, "It is bad enough to fly halfway around the world to see your daughter, and then she doesn't even recognize you when she walks in the door."

We all turned around at the same time to see my father and his co-pilot standing there with their paperwork. I let out a yell so loud the whole building echoed. I ran over to him and gave him the most prominent, longest hug he had ever had. An Air Force officer came out of the back room to see what all the commotion was about and just turned around and returned to his office. Dad's first officer took the paperwork from him and went out the door, leaving us there together. The four of us spent just a few minutes together before we decided it was time to depart. My father gave me one more big hug and followed us out the door.

He walked over to his aircraft and climbed the truck stairs to the front passenger door where a couple of flight attendants were waiting for him. We walked over to our aircraft and started the preparation for our mission. I turned and waved to him as his 747 made a turn off the tarmac and taxied to the runway. Both of us watched as it started its roll down the runway, slowly reaching for the thin air. It made a right turn after leaving us behind and pointed its nose towards Frankfurt. Air traffic control wished him a safe flight. The first officer replied that they would see them in a couple of days.

As I watched him disappear into the horizon. Deep in my mind I felt that I was a big girl now and a big part of a war. My father had fought his battle and most likely was still fighting it. He seldom talked about it, but D.D. always said, "When your father decides to spend time sitting on that cottonwood stump, don't disturb him. He is fighting his war."

I saw my father one more time in Riyadh Air Base operations. His crew and our crew were both collecting our flight plans. Just before the ground assault into Kuwait and Iraq began.

The second time he stayed longer than the first. My father asked if I had any information on Jim or had even talked to him. Sadly I had to say, "No." I had not spoken with him since his squadron departed in October. Other than Jim, we talked about Christmas being just a little bit quieter than usual. Mark and Judy were there with Judy's parents. They would be graduating from veterinary school in June. Hopefully, this war would be over by then, and I would make it home.

For six weeks the air campaign carried on with no end in sight. Then it all of a sudden became busier on February 23.

One night we heard that a VF-14 was down in our vector. The crew had bailed out before it went down. Our P-3C team had detected a GPS signal from the downed aircraft crew. We also noticed Iraqi military ground movement nearby, and the rescue choppers 20 minutes away from rescuing the crew. The race was on to be there first.

Betsy's team was listening in on the conversations. We could hear the worried voice of the VF-14 leader. Finally, Betsy said with a smile, "Let's give those Iraqi's something to think about." I was at the weapons control board and I entered the position code given me by the radar crew in the back into the harpoon missile. I then released the projectile, hoping it would hit the target. The board crew followed its path to the target.

Our chief yelled at the VF-14 crew to, "Hit the dirt!" Less than a minute later, the sky lit up. After that the scene went quiet except for a couple of choppers coming in to the crew's rescue. Ten minutes later, the crew was rescued and returning to their ship. Betsy looked over at me and with a smile, "Did you recognize that voice?"

"It sounded like Jim for a moment," I replied.

Betsy made a quick turn and started climbing back into the evening stars. "He owes us."

Business was as usual in the cockpit for the next several duty hours. Just another day at work for these ladies and their crew. Women were not allowed in the combat area, but women were flying choppers and were in other support operations.

Surprisingly the Desert Storm ground war was over in five days—the final cease-fire reached in April. The 4 P-3Cs continued their surveillance until then. When the ceasefire was signed, orders came down from Naval headquarters that all but 2 P-3Cs would be returning to their original bases. Betsy and her crew would be returning to Whidbey.

My father was becoming a regular fixture on the air force base when he came to pick up troops and return them to the United States. His company painted a large yellow ribbon on each side of the aircraft. Just beneath the cockpit was Desert Storm 1 painted in large black letters. I managed to get a picture of it as it was reaching for the horizon one afternoon.

Since the Whidbey crew was the first crew on sight in Saudi Arabia and I had not arrived until two months later, I felt I would not be returning to Whidbey like Betsy and the rest of the team. Then orders came down for all of us, and it was not to return to Whidbey as we initially thought. We were to transfer to Diego Garcia to await further orders. Betsy had heard through the rumor mill that some special operations were happening in Asia, but nothing else was coming down.

23

MONITORING DRUG MOVEMENT

As the sun was rising in the East, we left Saudi Arabia for Diego Garcia, an island out in the middle of the Indian Ocean. It was a Navy base that became very important during the Vietnam War. During Desert Storm, it became a B-52 staging area. Being a Navy base, it would feel better than the Air Force base we left behind. The six hour flight was mainly over water. The original crew without me had made this same track to the Middle East with other P-3C aircrafts when Iraq invaded Kuwait. They had a couple of new systems onboard the plane, and when called had been in the Pacific Theater testing them. The sun was beginning to set as I, sitting in the number 2 seat, requested permission to land. All day long we could see only water out of our windows with only a ship once in a while.

The landing was smooth since Betsy began her descend over 10 miles out. A flight officer met us shortly after we completed our check of the aircraft. He welcomed us and showed us all to our quarters. The commanding officer would see us in the morning. Whatever the mission was, it seemed like there was no hurry in letting us know. The entire crew spent time walking the beach before eating dinner at the officers' mess.

Betsy and Nancy finally let me know that the officer I replaced was also a Prowler pilot. It did not take the Navy long to transfer him back into that squadron, which was also a Whidbey squadron. Betsy explained to me that she felt that I would be upset if I figured it out. I smiled at Betsy and thanked her for being honest with me. Then I explained that my parents cautioned me shortly after graduating from the Naval Academy that sometimes second best becomes a better choice than originally you thought. I explained to Betsy that being with her gave me an insight into being a leader, and I thanked her for mentioning me to the commanders to see if I could join her crew. "I've enjoyed being part of the entire crew. I only hope I was able to add something worthwhile to all of you." Betsy assured me that I had, and thanked me for agreeing to join the crew.

The following day while the whole crew was enjoying breakfast, the base commander joined us at the table. We all stood at attention as he came over to the table and requested to sit with us. We then invited him to be seated, and he asked us to relax. "This is both business and personal. First, let us get personal. I've heard quite a bit about this crew and your actions in the Middle East. Before then, I also learned of your actions chasing drug traffickers on the West Coast."

He handed us two folders which contained photos and a copy of a secure email identifying images of ships. Both ships were container ships either completely loaded or partially loaded with containers. Each email gave the ship's name, owner, origination, and presumed destination. The email also identified the cargo that was on board. The crew looked at the officer who was at the end of the table. Since Betsy was the leader, she asked the first question, "What are we supposed to do with this information?"

"The ship that is not quite loaded yet will be stopping in Shanghai to finish out the cargo. The other one is stopping in Japan, and we believe it is transporting drugs from Indonesia. That one is not loading any cargo, but they are unloading a dozen containers. You will be flying to Atsugi from here with a layover in Singapore.

"The ship leaving Jakarta stops in Japan, but only to unload specific containers. The real problem is that our people want to know where they are loading the drugs. When they docked in Los Angles a few months back, the dogs could sniff the dope, but their handlers could not find any. So we need to track that ship until we know where it loads and unloads the drugs. Since it only docks in Japan for a few hours, their customs do not come on board the ship. Once we locate the loading zone, your crew can proceed to Japan and layover until we know when the other ship leaves Shanghai.

"The ship leaving Shanghai will be tracked by P-3Cs from Atsugi until it goes beyond their range. Between the two missions, you should return to Whidbey around June 1. When the second ship leaves Japan, make your destination Whidbey and request fueling somewhere along the Alaskan Coast. Both the Canadian and American authorities have requested your assistance in this manner since your crew was in the Middle East and you have done this type of surveillance before. Your team came to someone's attention in Seattle."

"When are we supposed to leave your island and start tracking this ship that is leaving Jakarta?" Betsy asked.

"You will leave Diego Garcia tomorrow morning and fly to Singapore, where you will wait until an embassy officer alerts you to the departure time of the ship from Jakarta. The Singaporean authorities know that you are coming; they will accommodate your mission. Spend the rest of the day getting a suntan and leave tomorrow morning at 0600." The commander smiled at them as he left and wished them, "Good luck hunting."

The sun was rising when we left Diego Garcia the following day. It was five and one-half hours to Singapore, arrival in the early evening. An embassy official and a second gentleman met us as we taxied to the private parking area at the International Airport. A customs official and the two gentlemen from the embassy all boarded the aircraft. The customs officer checked our papers and left. The two embassy personnel stayed on board to have a private briefing with the crew.

One of them handed us a folder with information and documents stating our mission. Our target would be leaving the harbor in eight hours, moving up our original departure time by one day. As a result, all three pilots would be taking turns flying. The instrument crew would be doing the same until tracking the target was no longer needed. We would be leaving in less than six hours for Jakarta. Each crew member studied the folder.

We drew straws to see who would take the four cots for the first three hours of sleep. The three pilots and one enlisted crew member would take the first shift. It was my responsibility to make sure the required fuel was onboard for the mission. Shortly after I had signed off on the fuel slip, I did one more pre-check of the entire plane. The two embassy personnel stood by in an automobile, ensuring no one came close to the aircraft. Since very few people knew of the tracking device that was new to the plane, keeping people away was a good thing.

Betsy let me take the first shift as the pilot of the aircraft just before we left Singapore. We went through all of our pre-trip checks before I requested tower permission for taxi and takeoff. After the tower granted permission and wished us well, I taxied the aircraft to the runway.

As we waited for a larger aircraft to land, I was surprised to see it was my father's company's 747. Halfway around the world, the sight gave me the satisfaction that my father was near and watching over me. We took off and made a hard right turn setting our destination for Jakarta, approximately five hours away.

Once reaching the assigned altitude we fanned the number 1 and 4 engines for fuel savings. There was a full moon out, with the stars making their beauty noticeable in the surrounding universe. Even though this was not supposed to be a dangerous mission, it was still a strange part of the world for seasoned veterans so far from their home shores. We were searching for a ship that had the habit of disappearing after it had dropped its cargo.

We entered Malaysian air space and notified their ATC that we would only be doing a training cruise along their coast. It was still early in the morning and the sun had not yet risen in the sky, but daylight was on the horizon in the east. Betsy had taken over the controls now as we filed for a lower attitude and started the number 1 and 4 engines to comply with the softer attitude. The crew in the back was monitoring the instruments. We finally reached the harbor of Jakarta, and found the object of our mission preparing to leave the port with a couple of tug boats escorting the large container ship away from the docks and beyond the traffic. We were on time and on target. So as not to be noticed, we decided to fly down the coast and then return farther out at sea.

Slowly we flew down along the coast, letting Malaysian ATC know that we were still on a training mission testing a new device. Returning to the harbor area, we found the target ship heading out to sea under its own power. Once again, we gained altitude so as not to be noticed by anyone. There seemed to be quite a bit of air traffic in the area, which provided some cover. We had watched for about two hours when a smaller boat pulled up alongside the ship.

The crew in the back right away identified it as a police patrol boat loaded heavily with cargo. It was a slow transfer of cargo from one to the other. Then the patrol boat moved away from the ship and made its way back to Jakarta. Before it reached its dock, the senior enlisted officer of our control board contacted a person in Jakarta. We hoped a reception party would be waiting for them! Then we returned our attention to the ship and followed it for about an hour until we knew it was out to sea.

The next destination was Atsugi in Japan, which was approximately 13 hours flying time. We had already used 9 hours of fuel and had to either return to Singapore or continue on to Japan, requesting a tanker to meet us somewhere in between. A message was forwarded to Naval headquarters Pacific requesting authorization to continue to Atsugi or return to Singapore. We still had our target ship in sight when the order came through: Continue to Atsugi, and there would be a tanker all ready waiting for us en route to refuel us.

The next stop was Atsugi, so Betsy notified the crew at the boards of our destination. We continued to track the ship's progress until we could not. Being a military aircraft, we stayed well away from the Asian coast. With the new instruments on board, there was no way we wanted to be caught in a bad situation. The evening was starting to set when we made the final approached to Atsugi, another unknown stay similar to Diego Garcia. There was still one more ship that needed tracking; as far as we knew, it was still in a Chinese port.

When we landed, a Navy operations tower directed us to a parking space. Just like Singapore, there were two people in business attire meeting us. One of them was a woman this time. Both civilians worked their way up the stairs to the passenger door. A Navy seaman opened the door and welcomed us to the base. He informed us he would show us to our guest quarters once the two civilians had completed the debriefing.

They introduced themselves as drug enforcement agents at the same time showing us their ID from Seattle. Each proceeded to inform the crew how vital our mission was to them. They requested permission to listen to the recordings of the operation up to now. Even the patrol boat that met the ship at sea was on record and identified. The civilians handed us another folder that specified the ship leaving China, supposedly in two days. This one did not seem as significant as the first one. One exception was this ship was carrying illegal's who boarded via container in China. Hopefully, they had enough air to survive a two week voyage to Seattle. The ship was flying a Panamanian flag; the ownership was a Greek Company.

The squadron commander joined us for dinner one evening and informed us the ship had left China. Other than the illegal's, there were no civilians on board. Shortly after leaving, it had turned off its responder, but another was attached to its hull. Something was up, and the U.S. government wanted to know. One of their squadrons' aircraft had been keeping track of its progress. He also informed us the Malaysian ship we had followed had arrived in port early this morning, and one of their agents now had it under surveillance. It would leave within a few hours, and one of their squadron aircraft would follow it out to sea.

Our crew would leave approximately one day after the departure of the ships from their respective ports. Meanwhile, Atsugi's base squadron would follow both vessels. Our crew would then pick up the trail and Elmendorf Air Force base would supply a tanker en route.

Everything seemed to be going according to plan. It was early afternoon when we began to prepare the aircraft for departure. The sun was starting to set as we rolled into position for takeoff. The night sky over Japan was sort of surreal, with Mount Fujiyama towering over the beautiful scenery. Japanese air traffic control directed us towards departure from their airspace into international airspace. Our crew had already begun communicating with the other P-3Cs from the Atsugi squadron on the scene. We climbed to 35000 feet and fanned the numbers 1 and 4 props again to save fuel. There was a full moon out as Betsy assumed the left command seat of the aircraft. I was number 3 in line, so I tried to relax. My father always complained that returning to the U.S. on this trip was the worst. /Since leaving Riyadh, Saudi Arabia, we'd always been flying into the rising sun.

About four hours later we came upon one of the ships, and it wasn't long before the other appeared on our radar screens. We relieved Atsugi's P-3s as we came upon the second ship. The new instrument called the Outlaw that was so successful in Desert Storm was now doing its job in the Pacific. At daylight both ships were traveling neck and neck. The vessel that had left Jakarta with several bales of cargo on board moved about half of its shipment onto the vessel that had just left China. That ship's destination happened to be Tacoma, Washington, while the destination of the container ship we'd been following since Jakarta was Los Angeles, California. All of a sudden, this mission was starting to come together for us.

I moved into the number one position as Betsy joined the crew to watch the show, as she called it. We zeroed in on the operation as it progressed, which took maybe 60 minutes. Then both ships separated and moved on, one with its newly boarded cargo. Even though we were flying at 35000 feet with two engines fanned, our chief petty officer did not seem too concerned about being detected since there were at least seven other aircraft flying this route today.

"Now, what do we do since we've seen the transfer? Do we need to keep an eye on them for a while although we're in the middle of nowhere?" Betsy asked her crew.

I was the first to answer, "My father always talked about Shemya although I have no idea how far we are from there or what they have for services."

The chief petty officer made a quick calculation. "It is about 45 minutes from here."

Betsy quickly asked him to send the request to their squadron commander at Whidbey. It took about took 10 minutes to receive the authorization.

We promptly requested permission from Shemya Air Force Base to land, fuel, and maybe take a short layover. The reply came back with an affirmative and gave us the wind, temperature, and runway information. The last question they asked was, "Is this an emergency?"

Nancy the number two pilot replied it was not, but we were on a mission, and our commander at Whidbey would most likely contact them. I set the heading for the new destination and silently said to myself, "Thank you, Dad, for your help." The number 1 and 4 engines came back online as we lowered our attitude and prepared to approach Shemya Air Force Base.

Everybody had their eyes glued to the windows. The island was surrounded by water, with a few steel buildings placed around the base. It was defiantly isolated, and it was daylight. Then Betsy remembered it was June, and this part of the world was not far from having 24 hours of daylight.

Shortly after landing we taxied to a parking area directed by their traffic control. One of our aircraft's petty officers opened the door and dropped the stairs; the base commander was standing there waiting for an invite to come onboard. He handed us a telex from Whidbey's commander to stand down for six hours and then pick up the mission as both ships approached the Alaskan coast. It also indicated that their satellite tracking system AIS was now up and running. The ships were about 100 miles apart at this time. One ship they'd been tracking since Jakarta was inching closer to the Alaskan coast. The other was more in a direct route to the U.S. coast.

The base commander invited all our crew to dinner in their mess. Regulations stated when in a non-Navy area, two members must stay with the aircraft for security reasons. As junior among the command crew, I stayed behind with the junior petty officer. I informed Betsy I would supervise the refueling of the aircraft. The junior petty officer would continue tracking both ships so as to be ready when we continued the mission. He took this mission very seriously and was the only petty officer onboard that had trained on The Outlaw.

Eventually the rest of the crew returned and relieved us. Betsy informed me that the commanding officer was holding our table. The junior petty officer and I made our way over to the mess hall. Neither of us had eaten since leaving Japan, so a sit-down meal was welcome. We picked up our meal and the colonel motioned us over to his table. We introduced ourselves and began a small conversation as the two of us ate dinner. The officer gave me a questioning look and asked, "You are Larry Becker's daughter, aren't you?"

I looked at him, not surprised. "Yes. How did you guess?"

"Well, a good question, young lady. Your father and I go way back to Vietnam. He and I were in prison at the same time."

Once again my curiosity took hold. I questioned him about how come he was in command here. "Well, young lady, my wife divorced me while I was in prison, and our two children grew up without their dad. They consider their stepfather as their father now. So I just plain stayed in the service. I could not fly anymore, so I've found assignments no one else wanted. This island was one of them. I've been here for two years. Once a month, I send in a report. We take care of any military flights like yours, or commercial flights a couple of times a week. Believe it or not, until your father started flying military flights in the Middle East, I talked with him a couple of times a month. He invited me to his ranch this summer when I return to the mainland on leave, so I most likely will take him up on the invitation." It was time to get back to our aircraft, so I wished him good luck and let him know I might see him if he were to come to the ranch.

Finally, it was time to leave, and the ground personnel gave us the all-clear sign and flagged us off. Ground control then directed us to the only runway. Even though it was 2300 on the following day, there was still very much daylight. Nancy, the number 2 pilot, was at the controls as the aircraft began rolling and taking off over the Pacific. The chief petty officer had already located our target so those numbers were installed in the automatic pilot that would fly the aircraft. As we attained 35,000 feet, Nancy fanned two engines. Below us lay several ships and a few smaller fishing boats. Our craft seemed to be making perfect time since we had left them over 7 hours ago. The ship we were following stayed about 30 miles offshore. The other ship, the one that had stopped in China, was over 200 miles offshore, making way to its destination.

We caught up to our target as it stood at a standstill just outside of Cook Inlet. Another boat was pulling up beside it and started taking on cargo from the larger ship. Our P-3C circled the action at 35,000 feet so we could get a good video. One clip gave us a good photograph of the boat taking on cargo. It gave us suitable identification and the size of the presumed fishing trawler. They stayed together for almost 30 minutes before separating and continuing in their respective directions. The boat accepting the cargo was returning up Cook Inlet towards Anchorage. The larger one started up and continued to move out to sea away from the coastline. We sent the information to the DEA (Drug Enforcement Administration) offices in Seattle.

It was still early morning in Seattle and the DEA offices were not yet close to opening. Betsy and her crew were left wondering what to do since we had not heard from Seattle. The chief petty officer's most experienced team member felt calling the Coast Guard should be done now instead of later. He said, "Tell the Coast Guard to keep this under wraps until the head office of the DEA in Seattle notifies them. I am sure that they don't want this to get out until all of the cargo has been delivered."

Just as Betsy was calling the Coast Guard, a teletype message popped up on the screen. "Keep the evidence. Our people in Anchorage have the matter in hand." Everyone relaxed as they continued following the ship as it now proceeding farer off the coast.

Both ships still were on the aircraft's radar as another telex came through from the commander of Whidbey Island Naval Air Station. "Proceed to Whidbey. You are being relieved of duty and replaced.

Welcome home." It had been a long month chasing ships across the Pacific. We had accomplished much in war and now in peace. I looked at Betsy and Nancy with a smile and mentioned, "It will be nice being in my own bed tonight."

Betsy looked at both of us and said, "It will be nice to be in bed with my honey!"

We all laughed when the chief petty officer from the back came over the microphone, "Ladies, watch what you wish. It might be more than either one of you can handle."

We tagged along above the ship that had just dropped its cargo off on the fishing boat until we were relieved by the Canadian team. Then Nancy set the autopilot for Whidbey and home. After that, it was housekeeping time with the evidence collected over the last month. All the information we had was organized and stored for the drug enforcement people. It would take us the rest of the flight to complete this duty. I went back to help them work on the project since I was just passing time watching the scenery go by from my flight engineer's seat in the cockpit.

24

RETURNING TO WHIDBEY

All of us looked out the windows as we approached Vancouver Island and started the descent for landing. Betsy asked me to take the left seat for landing. "We all are happy that you decided to join us last fall; besides that, you have been a great friend and companion to all of us. We would have had to return to Japan if you hadn't thought of Shemya. The professionalism you have shown tells all of us what kind of a person and officer you are."

I smiled as I climbed into the left seat and replied, "Let's go home and have fun."

It was a good feeling when I set the aircraft down on the Whidbey runway. I reversed the props to slow the process down as we approached the taxiway and pulled into our parking area as directed by base operations. Our ground crew had returned weeks before and proceeded to park and check the aircraft. Shortly after all engines had been shuttered, a crowd descended on us. Our chief petty officer opened the door and released the hidden stairs. I almost forgot to signal to the ground control leader as I saw Jim standing among the crowd with a big smile. We hadn't talked or even seen each other since he'd left with his squadron last fall.

Hurrying, we completed all the paperwork. Some men in civilian clothes were the first to board and wanted to have a briefing with us. The chief petty officer and Betsy presented them with all the files we had accumulated since leaving the Middle East. Betsy felt the whole ordeal was necessary, but seemed to have taken forever. The base commander informed us that we would have one day off, so enjoy it. Meanwhile, one of the other P-3s would keep track of both ships.

Finally, the entire crew emerged from the aircraft to the patiently waiting group of families and friends. We were the last of Whidbey's squadrons to return from the Middle East. The entire crew, with our duffle bags, descended the aircraft stairs.

None of us even knew what day it was, much less what time. While the ground crew towed the plane to the hangar, I dropped my duffle bag and ran into the arms of Jim. I could tell he wasn't expecting it, but he was delighted with my reaction. He picked up my duffle bag, and together with Greg and Betsy walked to Jim's car hand in hand. "The men will be cooking dinner tonight at my house," as Greg informed us.

The Cascade Mountains and clear skies were the order of the day. Across Puget Sound, the Olympics were putting on their best show. The guys dropped us at our apartment first to change into civilian clothes and maybe take good hot showers. It was something we both needed. At the same time, the guys did some grocery shopping for dinner.

Leaving Riyadh, Saudi Arabia, we had been living on the aircraft, even on layovers. The longest was in Japan. Diego Garcia had been just a few days. Shemya and Singapore had been the shortest layovers as we waited for orders or until our targets caught up with us. In Diego

Garcia we were able to play on the beach for a few hours. Sleeping and shower quarters felt better than the four cots in our aircraft. In Singapore we stayed with the aircraft, only wishing we could see the city. I had been there with my parents and loved it. Shemya was the most interesting for me; my father had mentioned it once in a while. Meeting an old friend of my father's there was certainly something I had not expected.

Since Greg had already mentioned that Betsy was staying with him, I asked Betsy if Jim could spend the night with me. Betsy took a long look at me and asked, "Have you ever slept with a man before, mister."

I hesitated before answering her. "No, I haven't, and I am still a virgin if you must know."

"Joni, since you care for Jim like I think you do, you are going to be in for one beautiful experience."

I had a shy smile when I replied, "I guess that means yes." We hugged each other and continued getting ready for the guys to return.

The guys returned with the groceries. We ladies were ready. Both of the guys were standing in the entryway when we made our entrance. "Man, now I know what that song meant about the lady in those tight-fitting jeans." Jim had a smile across his face as he made the comment. Greg looked at Betsy and let her know that she would not be coming home for the evening.

"Wow!" Jim looked at Greg and never said another word.

Greg had a beautiful home overlooking Puget Sound. He was also one great cook. Jim's background in cooking was beef and trout, but Greg was good at seafood. So that is what we would have this afternoon. Both guys liked each other. Since they had been dating roommates, they had become friends. Greg had season football tickets and shared baseball tickets with others in his office. Jim liked both but was too busy flying for an airline and the Navy Reserve to have much time for attending games. Greg did his time in the Marine Corps as a judge advocate. Since then, he was in the reserve but did not have to pull weekend duty like Jim.

We watched the sunset over the sound, the Olympics, and the San Juan Islands. Both couples decided to see if we could take a summer excursion and spend some time on the San Juan Islands. Betsy had heard of some great bed and breakfast establishments on Friday Harbor. Greg mentioned that he had traveled to Vancouver Island the fall before meeting Betsy and spent time there sightseeing. One of the fantastic sights he felt was the Butchart Gardens, which was beautiful that time of year.

It was late when Jim drove me home to my apartment. The outside light was on as we drove up into the parking space. He was the first to get out of the car with the thought of the long drive and ferry ride back to Everett. He opened the car door and escorted me to the door. It had been nine months since Jim had left me at the door.

Turning around and returning to his car, he heard me asked, "Do you think after not seeing you for nine months I am going to let you leave with just a kiss and hug? You are staying for the night after such a wonderful afternoon."

He gave me a long look with a stupid reply, "I guess I could use Betsy's bed."

I looked at him and shook my head, "No! You are staying in my bed, and we are sleeping together, my dear."

He looked at me from the end of the driveway, amazed that this was happening. "Aren't you forgetting something, mister? I am the senior officer here."

I smiled. "Well, I guess I am going to make love to a senior officer."

Smiling, he reached into the car, picked up his overnight bag, turned and walked back to the apartment.

"Your father is going to kill me." We both laughed and held each other close. Betsy was right about the evening being one I would remember for a long time.

The phone rang and I answered it. I was looking at the time and wondering why anyone would be calling this time of the morning. It was Betsy, and the first thing she asked was if Jim was still there. Jim rolled over with a groan about the same time. Betsy sort of laughed. "I guess it is the wrong question to ask this morning. We've been called back on duty at 0900. It appears our target is now approaching Vancouver Island. Another aircraft is on the tail of the San Francisco bound vessel. Greg is bringing me home so I can change into my flight suit."

Sleepily I replied, "Guess I better kick him out and get going." I hung up the phone and rolled over in bed.

Jim, with a smirk on his face, acknowledged he had to get going. "Honey, it has been one hell of a night; if I haven't said it before, I will repeat it—I love you." He gave me a big hug and kissed me as if it would never end.

"You are still one great kisser, honey," I said as I rolled over and crawled out of bed.

Jim departed before Betsy arrived home. I was eating some hot oatmeal that was leftover when we left last fall. Betsy changed into her flight suit and grabbed a cup of coffee before we hurriedly went out the door. Twenty minutes later, we pulled into the hangar parking lot and entered the operations office where the rest of the crew was waiting. The chief petty officer had already gathered the paperwork, when the operations commander informed us to go right to the briefing room. The squadron commander met us there and filled us in on the mission at hand. He then opened a door and invited three other people into the room.

We were all introduced to each other. Then the commander proceeded to advise us that each of them belonged to a different organization. DEA, FBI, and customs representatives would be joining us on this mission. The ship Betsy's team left behind yesterday at the Cook Inlet. It entered Canadian Waters dropped some more cargo onto another cruiser before continuing into US Waters.

The Royal Canadian Mounted Police would join the Coast Guard in intercepting the ship after it made the Canadian drop. The DEA officer seemed to know that the pickup boats were stationed in Neah Bay. One of his team had just notified him that pickup boats were preparing to leave the dock. Betsy looked over at her crew and requested the squadron's permission to get started on the mission. The chief petty officer and his enlisted personnel had already done their pre-check and supervised the fueling of the P-3C.

Our crew and guests left the briefing room and proceeded to the hangar area. The aircraft and the rest of the team was waiting for us. I did the pilot's last pre-check of the aircraft. Then I boarded the plane and closed the passenger door behind me. Nancy and I assumed the pilots seats and Betsy informed us that she was taking the command and would keep herself free doing the engineers/weapons control officer jobs.

I notified the ground control personnel, "Brakes set," after sitting in the left seat. Slowly number two inside engine started to turn with one, three and four to follow.

Nancy signaled to the ground crew, "Engines started, pull the air and power." The ground crew obliged, then informed her that they would be giving the wave off. We followed the flagger out to the taxiway and the wave off on the left. The two pilots were still doing their check-offs as we reached the runway and waited for the control tower to release us as an E-6 Prowler was landing. After that, it was all business among the entire aircraft crew as we began the takeoff.

Slowly the P-3C reached for the air as the landing gear retracted in the belly. The target ship's location was installed into the autopilot system. ATC released the aircraft to 20,000 feet after we gave our destination per the GPS. It was less than thirty minutes before we had the ship on the radar screen. It also showed a couple of other vessels coming out of Neah Bay, Washington as the DEA agent had noted in the briefing room. Betsy and the chief petty officer both agreed that the meeting place was still about an hour out.

Betsy ordered the flight crew to set up an observation area within an approximately 60 mile radius. I quickly did the math, passed it onto Nancy and she set the autopilot with the information. The two Coast Guard craft could be seen on the screen, each staying approximately thirty miles from the scene. Slowly the operation began to take place between the ship and the two vessels meeting it. Betsy ordered us to move closer and take us down to 10,000 feet. Finally, the ship came to a halt, drifting in the waters of the Pacific Ocean just inside Puget Sound where the water was less choppy. Then the other two vessels pulled up beside the larger vessel. The entire crew in the back started to record the happenings as our guests watched and discussed the whole operation. Then the smaller vessels pulled away from the larger container vessel and began their journey into Neah Bay.

A welcoming party would be waiting for them when they arrived. Since the San Francisco part of this operation had not been taken down but would happen later this evening, the authorities decided to let the vessel continue on its way to Tacoma so as not to alert the its owners to the operation that just happened in Neah Bay. Betsy made the decision to stay with the smaller vessels as they began their journey toward shore. Once again, she advised the crew to stay more out to sea so as not to alert their targets that they were being watched and recorded. Trying not to look suspicious, the authorities began to move closer to the vessels.

Our chief petty officer yelled through the headset that one of the vessels had turned away from the other. It was moving very fast, and it looked like the Coast Guard vessel could not catch it. At the same time the other vessel continued onto its destination. The DEA agents on board our aircraft was wondering what they could have seen that the other boat had not.

I asked Betsy if she minded me doing some fancy flying to stop the vessel from making its way farther away from the action. Betsy gave me a questioning look and finally said, "The aircraft is yours. Just don't get us in trouble."

I then asked Nancy to start counting off the attitude changes as I started to go down towards the water. Betsy yelled into the headset for everyone to be seated and fasten their seat belts as a fighter pilot was in charge for the time being. Everyone just laughed as the guests showed fear on their faces. Nancy lightly put both of her hands on the controls to cover me as I proceeded with the maneuver.

Looking out the right window, the crew could see the vessel making a break for it just below them. Nancy was calling out numbers when I yelled, "Hold it." Both officers held it until they had passed the vessel and were ahead of it by a couple of miles. Slowly I made a left turn and then a right turn looking right straight at the boat. "Ok, start counting; we will hold at two hundred feet." By this time, Betsy had joined them in the cockpit with one of the customs officers. It looked like the boat was stopping or trying to maneuver away from a possible head-on collision with us. Just a bit lower we approached the vessel and then went right over the top of it as Nancy and I together pulled the aircraft out of its flight path, gaining attitude and making a left turn to return to the scene.

Everyone was laughing as we saw several figures in the water and a boat making circles around them. I was too busy trying to control the aircraft with Nancy's help to see what was happening. I was preparing to make another pass when the chief petty officer signaled that the cutter had arrived.

We left the cutter to figure out how to stop the boat from making circles in the water. "That was some magnificent flying miss. Where did you learn that?" asked the customs agent.

I smiled and replied, "I'm a Prowler pilot, but they won't let me fly combat because I am a woman. Then again, I have never enjoyed myself as much as I have the last several months with this crew and aircraft. We've been places that I would never have been if I was flying an Prowler. Every bit of it has been an adventure."

"I saw your last name on your flight suit, and I am wondering if you have a relative that flies for an airline out of Seattle and lives in Montana," the customs officer asked. Sitting in the pilot's seat and acting kind of surprise that my father's name even came up I replied, "Yes. That must be my father. We have a ranch in Montana."

"Tell your father that today we are in the process of closing the drug operation that began on one of his flights."

"All right, he will like that," I answered him.

I made one final turn when Betsy advised us that we could now return to Whidbey. This mission was now complete. It was a mission that began in the Middle East when we received orders for Diego Garcia. We had no idea it was another mission we were going on—a mission that took us almost halfway around the world before returning to our base.

Many others were part of the mission along the way including the person in Jakarta who informed his contacts when the ship was leaving, the embassy personnel in Singapore who spent time with us at the airport and then the squadron in Japan which took up the watch while we waited until it was our turn again.

I had felt I would be staying behind in the Middle East to pick up the slack for some other crew, but had remained with this crew. Betsy had put the word in for me to come and help, I had accepted the challenge and I had finally been in a war zone, although it had scared me. I had been ready for it. Like my father, I was now a veteran of Desert Storm. However, the most crucial mission, I came to understand, was the one we had just completed.

We soon landed and taxied our aircraft to the hangar tarmac. Upon arrival, the squadron commander ordered us to report to the briefing room for a debriefing before being released from duty.

The entire crew entered the briefing room with their guests. There to meet us were another member of the FBI and another of the DEA. They explained their reason for being there and wanted everyone to know the story behind today's mission and its origins back in Jakarta. As the customs agent indicated to me, it had been an ongoing case for the last few years.

"It began when a passenger on an incoming passenger flight had a briefcase full of pure heroin. Before today it had taken the lives of two customs agents. First, there was a customs undercover agent executed in his garage. The other agent died because of his pure stupidity. The operation had taken its toll on other agents as well. Today drug lords in Malaysia and others of the cartel are being rounded up. By the time this day ends, many of the cartels' members here in the U.S. and Malaysia will be in Jail.

"The kingpin was arrested just a few hours ago in Jakarta. It appears that your surveillance paid off when you discovered that a police vessel was transporting the heroin from a warehouse in Jakarta out to the ship after it had left the port. Your team had been doing an awe-inspiring job on earlier missions. We requested for you to do the surveillance since your team had done it before leaving for the Middle East. Your crew was in the right place at the right time, and we needed someone with experience. Thanks, captain!"

Betsy then stood up and thanked the people in the room commenting, "My crew deserves the thanks, if not for them and sharing the responsibility and their experience we would not have been able to do this."

There was a certain peace between Betsy and me as we gathered up our gear. Together we went back to the aircraft for one last sight. As we did one more walk around, Betsy said with a smile, "This old girl has seen a lot of action in the previous year. It is time for her to go in and get some significant maintenance done on her.

"I think it is about time for us to take a breather for a spell. Greg and I are going to spend some time with our parents and maybe even get married. Just wondering, would like to be my maid of honor, Joni?"

It caught me off guard, but my answer was a resounding, "Yes!"

"The prowler commander wants you back in his squadron as soon as you take some time off," Betsy mentioned to me.

"I never really thought about it since I had a great experience with your team," I replied to Betsy. "You and your crew have taught me so much in the last several months it will be hard to move on."

Betsy just smiled as she replied, "Let us go home, but first stop at the grocery store and pick up some food for the bare refrigerator and just relax for the first time in months with that beer you're buying."

We walked out of the hangar with Nancy to find the rest of our crew waiting for us. So instead of a salute, it was one big hug fest, with all of us knowing we would really enjoy the time off.

Next it was on to the base's PX, and then to the apartment, where we had not spent much time in the last nine months. It was a home to both of us, far from the rigors of Navy life. I felt I better call my parents before settling down to dinner. I had a feeling my brother was graduating from veterinary school in Pullman, Washington, but I had no idea when. D.D. answered the phone and was delighted to hear my voice.

She informed me that my father was out on a trip and would return early in the morning in a couple of days. He had talked with Jim, and they were driving to Pullman together from Seattle. I was surprised because I knew nothing about that. Then I laughed inside at myself because I had just kicked Jim out of the house this morning.

"Have you seen Jim at all since you've returned?" D.D. asked. I sat there on the phone, flabbergasted and stuttering—D.D. is just like a mother that knows all. "Ah! You have seen him, and he probably forgot to fill you in on the details." Well, nothing like being embarrassed by your stepmother.

I promised I would call Jim after we had dinner and said, "Goodbye and love you."

Together Betsy and I made dinner including Dungeness crab from the PX and a glass of wine from the Pacific Northwest. Just about the time we finished our first homemade dinner in months, the telephone rang. Betsy answered it and then gave me the phone with a smirk. "It is for you. Some guy named Jim."

The first thing out of his mouth was an apology: He forgot to tell me about Mark's graduation and that my dad was riding over with us. "Didn't you think maybe I should know about the plans?" I questioned him?

"Well, when you got called out this morning I did not know how long you would be gone. When the most beautiful girl in the world invites you into her bed for the night you have a habit of forgetting a whole lot."

"Lame excuse for a senior officer," I kidded him back.

After two good nights of rest, I drove down to Jim's place. Together, we went to the airport to pick my father up. He was sitting out on the sidewalk with a book waiting patiently for us. He had been up all night flying and needing some rest; the back seat became his domain. Before we even left Seattle, he was sound asleep.

25

MARK'S GRADUATION

Jim and I shared a couple of cute remarks between ourselves as the miles flowed beneath us. Finally, several hours later, when we arrived in Pullman, my father began to wake up.

In late afternoon D.D. pulled into the motel parking lot. She was pulling a sizable rental trailer with her one-ton pickup. She, Mark and Judy had been discussing all along about them moving back to Montana. Mark and Judy would assume Dakota's small ranch and turn it into a veterinary clinic for small and large animals. The three felt it was perfect being close to a major highway with a covered arena.

I have rarely seen my father at a loss for words. But this was one of those times. Jim just looked at him and slyly remarked, "Well Larry, it looks like the women in your family are full of surprises these days."

My father looked at Jim with a kind smile on his face. "Jim, if you stick around long enough, you will find out a lot more about these two women in this family."

"I already have Larry," Jim said, giving him the thumbs up like pilots do with each other when one takes over from the other. Jim had already come to admire the family. He was back two months prior to me and had called my family to fill them in on what I was doing. My father hadn't seen me since Riyadh, Saudi Arabia. One of base's commanding officers had advised him that I was on my way back to Whidbey, but that it might take a while since my crew was on a special unknown mission somewhere out in the Pacific.

Judy's family was staying at the same motel. D.D. had invited Roberts's family over also. So it looked like it was going to be a great big party around the pool. I worried about it and mentioned my concerns to D.D. "Don't worry about it because his fiancée will be with him. His brother will also be here with his fiancée, which I believe is your good friend Liz. They are planning a big wedding for both couples." Seeing Liz and even Robert was going to be interesting. I last saw Liz eight months ago when she had met me in Germany and taken me to Riyadh. Since then, I had not had too much time to find out how my friend was doing.

All the mothers had managed to find a caterer for dinner. With many phone calls they managed to get a menu together and line up a live band. The motel was full of their families and guests for the graduation ceremonies the next day. D.D. and Robert's mother stood at the door that evening and made name tags for the families and friends. The dinner was terrific, and everyone enjoyed each other's company.

Before dinner, Robert walked over to me and introduced his fiancée. She was a teacher and had just received her master's degree. I could tell right off that she was going to be a great teacher. Liz wanted to sit next to me so we could catch up on each other. She had stayed in the Middle East and still made her rounds to all the Navy carriers delivering mail and other items they needed at sea. She was home on a month's leave, so she and John decided to make it a double wedding with Robert and his fiancéé. Each of the fathers made a toast to the graduates and wished them well.

Dinner finished, several couples started dancing to the music, including Jim and me. My father and stepmother danced and acted like a couple of college sweethearts. Then, surprising everyone, she asked her husband if he would play the piano for the crowd.

The piano player decided he needed a drink and let my father take his place. He started playing some of Floyd Cramer and Roger williams music. When the sax player figured out what my father was playing, he joined in. The music was slow and romantic for the warm evening mood. I had heard my father play before, but tonight seemed so different. Jim could feel something going on with me that he had never seen before tonight. There were tears in my deep brown eyes. He asked me to let him into my world. Gently I laid my head on his chest. "My mother is here tonight playing her piano opposite of him. When I was a little girl, I can remember that they together would play the most beautiful music that I had ever heard."

Mark saw the tears in my eyes. He and Judy moved over next to us. He put his arm around me and held me close. D.D. noticed the hug that Mark was giving me and the tears in both of our eyes. She walked over to us, realizing that her stepchildren still missed their mother. "Your mother is here, isn't she?" D.D. asked.

Mark and I both nodded our heads, "Yes."

"Your father needs his family." Dakota grabbed both of our hands and led us over to the piano. We all put our hands on him as he continued to play. We could see the tears in his eyes. Jim had spent enough time with him the last couple of years to realize what was happening.

Many in their airline family had told the story of Larry Becker and his wife Eve. Most felt that there was something exceptional between them. They both worked for the airline and were well-liked by everyone they encountered. Jim reached over and held my free hand tight; as Judy saw what Jim was doing, she did the same with Mark. As our father continued playing, the band kept up the pace he was setting. The music was beautiful, rising out of love and respect. The audience became enchanted and just stood there, finally feeling the love in this family. It was perfect for a warm summer evening with all the stars and a full moon out.

My father finally finished the last piece and motioned to the regular piano player to take over. He rose from the bench and the whole family hugged for a couple of minutes in silence. "I am sorry for spoiling your festive evening," my father apologized to his family.

D.D. was the first to speak up, "You spoiled nothing. Tonight you made us all feel what love is." Everyone else in the huddle felt the same.

Jim looked at me, Mark and Judy. "Let us not let this great music go to waste." All of our family and many other couples returned to the dance floor after the impromptu concert.

The next morning breakfast was also served by the pool. It was one of those warm sunny days in Eastern Washington, with a breeze coming in off the wheat fields of the Palouse. Graduation would take place at 2 PM outside in the Cougar football stadium. Over 400 graduates would receive their degrees—Mark and Judy would receive their Doctorate of Veterinary Medicine degrees.

The next adventure for them would be setting up their practice and getting married. I wondered how hard it was for my father to see his children grow up and leave the nest, looking back on all of the family times they'd had over the years. He had retired from the Navy and still had a ways to go with the airlines, and D.D. was also successful in her profession.

Again last night I saw my father in a different light. I knew my mother and he had loved music, and in early childhood memories I still can hear them playing their respective pianos. D.D. always said that my mother would always be there, and last night proved her right.

Mark and I always felt privileged to have two great mothers in our lives. Deep down, I realized from my father's reaction last night that after all of these years, he still loved our real mother, and knew that she was there with him last night playing the other piano. How D.D. handled the whole situation and turned it into something special surprised me. There was no jealousy when she suggested to us that our father needed both of them.

Jim and I discussed it for a long time before finally drifting off to sleep. Even though I was in love with Jim and knew he felt the same way, it took me a while to figure out that Jim and my father had a special connection. They had many long hours with each other in their time together in the cockpit.

Jim was a good listener, and tonight he was even more special. "Your family is exceptional, Joni. Tonight, just watching them and especially your stepmother was amazing. So many women I know would have made a scene in front of everyone. D.D. knew in a moment that something was amiss when she saw you and your brother together. She came over and informed you two that your father needed his family. She has known for more than 20 years that she can never replace your father's love for your mother. Your father had loved another woman, and still, she seemed to encourage all of you to keep remembering her." Jim held me close as he made that statement.

"Your father and I have had many conversations between ourselves on the long hauls. He is proud of all of you. His love for D.D. is extraordinary, and I only hope that someday you and I will have what they have."

I looked at him thoughtfully. "You know what you just said, don't you?"

He smiled and gave her one of his best kisses. "Yes, I do. Like your parents, I feel there is something very special between us."

Breakfast the following day was again served around the pool. Robert and John's parents were seated with my parents. Liz and John were alone at their table, so I joined them. We had all sat together the prior evening, so we all knew each other. All of them seemed to be interested in Jim's profession. He was now flying the left seat on the 747, which John seemed amazed could even fly. Jim's flying had been mainly in Asia. It was a strange place for John, who was just starting to travel beyond Texas. Like most people I've met over the years, John was excited to learn about Jim's many exotic destinations.

A baseball team in Japan had made some overtures to John while he was still in college. He had played winter ball in Florida this past winter and now was on the Orioles' roster. It wasn't only John who was interested in Jim's profession. Jim was also interested in John's as Jim was a sports fan. John being on the Orioles' roster was an outstanding achievement as well. Then I started wondering why Liz was still in Europe and the Middle East. She said that she was enjoying herself there and was looking forward to returning. John and Liz were anxious to hear about me chasing drug movements halfway around the globe.

With breakfast completed, we asked John and Liz if they would like to ride with us to the ceremonies in the afternoon. The afternoon was warm, and the shade of the stadium cover was excellent. It reminded

Liz and me of our graduation from the Academy, which seemed so long ago.

When it was all over, Mark's and Judy's families made their way to the apartment they had shared for the last two years. It did not take long for the two families to clean out the apartment and load all their belongings into the trailer which D.D. had rented after she arrived in Pullman. My father and D.D. were driving together back to Montana with the truck and trailer.

One more night in the motel, and the following day the caravan began its journey to Montana. Finally, we would be returning to our homes on the coast. Jim and I were taking August off this year; Jim was now flying a schedule so we could make plans in advance. I knew I would be back on the Prowler very soon. My commander wanted to have a conversation with me after I returned from Mark's graduation.

26

RETURN TO WORK

We arrived back in Everett, Washington at Jim's home. Early in the evening, while crossing Washington State, Jim had informed me it was his turn to fix dinner. "I stocked up before I left, and tomorrow I have to fly, so alcohol is out for the evening."

I gave him a questioning look and asked, "What else is out?"

"You are a devil, young lady, and I love you for it," he kidded.

Dinner was salmon with a sweet honey taste, baked potatoes, green beans and salad. It surprised me that he knew how to cook a great meal without wine while I relaxed on his deck, enjoying the end of a tiring day, and wondering if my family was home yet.

I finally had time to think of many other things. I hadn't seen D.D.'s ranch since being a child and experiencing sleepovers with her niece. I was now wondering how Mark and Judy were going to enjoy it. D.D. had it remodeled several times over the years and had enclosed the covered arena. My father had been there several times over the years, adding his touch to the many projects completed between renters moving in and out.

My thoughts were questioning what my base commander wanted to discuss with me. My last discussion with him was when I became a part of Betsy's crew in the Middle East, which had led to some exciting adventures. Those same thoughts reverted to Jim. We had spent 3 days together and we never discussed the war or our part in it.

I had not asked Jim if that crew we saved was his crew. Maybe someday when the time was right. I would tell him it was us that saved his crew from being captured, by the missile that came out of nowhere. That was for some other day when the time was right.

It would be late summer before we would all be together again. The times were getting further and further apart. I knew that someday Jim and I would be far apart because of our chosen professions. It had been nine months this last time when we were apart without any communication. Neither one of us had lost our feelings for each other.

I understood that my father would usually leave once a month for ten or eleven days each time. I also knew that my father and stepmother would be at most of Mark and my activities. He encouraged and supported all of us to follow our dreams, including D.D., who started writing books. It only took a few years for a couple of those books to be made into movies.

Jim made me breakfast before I left for Whidbey. Today I was going to take a ferry over to the island instead of driving around; I had never done this before. It was June, and Puget Sound was smooth on the short ferry ride between Mukilteo and Clinton. There was a recording from my commanding officer when I arrived home. He was inviting me to come to his office for a meaningful conversation. It wasn't quite 1300 yet, but I felt that it must be necessary if the squadron commander was calling.

I was dressed in my khakis when I made my way to the squadron commander's office. The receptionist asked me to wait in the reception room while the commander finished another appointment in his office. It was just a few minutes later when his door opened. As he bid goodbye to the officer that was leaving, I stood at attention because both officers were above my rank. Then he turned to me, returned the salute and invited me into his office.

"Please be seated," he said after escorting me into the office. "Many of your superiors have been speaking very highly of your skills, lieutenant. When your name came up last fall for a possible crew fill-in, you jumped at the chance and it only took you a couple of weeks to train for a different aircraft. Your group leader speaks very highly of your leadership skills. Your trainers in Texas and here felt inferior to you when they were with you.

"I noticed that you had all of your licenses even before you left the Naval Academy. The fact you could be out flying some commercial aircraft instead of flying for the Navy is something that some might overlook, but I don't." He sat forward in his oversized office chair and continued with what he was trying to get across. "You see, the lead training position is coming open in December, and many of us are wondering if you would like to take it. It would mean a promotion, and you would have to work with the present leader until then."

I sat there speechless; it must have seemed forever to my commanding officer. Then, once again, he spoke, "Lieutenant, are you still with me?"

"Yes, sir!" I finally replied. "I would be honored to lead the group, sir."

"Lieutenant, why don't you take a couple of weeks off before beginning your new assignment. Maybe even take a Prowler up for a few hours since it has been a while. I see you also put in for August off and if nothing is on the horizon, a couple weeks at Christmas is all right too."

I walked out of the office three miles high that warm June afternoon. I could not wait to call home that evening to fill my parents in on the news. But instead of returning to my empty apartment, I found an uninhabited beach. Just listening to the water as it rolled onto the shore and the sound of birds hunting for their prey was relaxing.

An older gentleman was working with a rake in different places, and I decided to go over and ask what he was doing. "Looking for oysters," he said as he held up the bucket he was carrying. Knowing that I was not from this area, he proceeded to show me how to find and shuck them. He then gave me a half dozen and then showed me how to cook them.

I thanked him and left for home with my prize and dinner for the evening. On the way home, I was thinking of the following day and trying to get acquainted with a new job. I felt good that they would give me six months to get the feel of it.

The oysters, cooked in some wine, tasted unbelievably great for my first taste of them. I finished up the wash I'd started earlier in the day and got ready for bed. As I was moving around the apartment, I saw the light on the phone blinking. It was a message from Jim wishing me a great week and that he loved me. Then almost forgetting, I decided to call my family.

Everyone was there, including Mark's fiancée, Judy, and her parents. My father had just come in from the hayfields, and Judy's father and Mark had returned from Mark and Judy's new home. D.D.'s cousin, who remodeled our home over 20 years ago, would take the job of remodeling D.D.'s old home. My father and D.D. sounded excited to hear I was now in the training department. They congratulated me, and wished me luck with those recent Navy male pilot graduates who knew everything. All of them had a good laugh at that one. Mark would be taking over the haying operation while dad was out on his next trip. It was a busy time in the ranching operation with branding a few weeks off. I wanted to be there with the family since I had missed so much during the last few years of Navy life.

When I hung up from the family and prepared for bed, a thought came to my mind: I'd call and made reservations for Great Falls, Montana. It would be a fun weekend, and I decided that the time away would be suitable for me to refresh my mind. I would ask Jim if he'd like to go when he returned from his ten day trip. He had already been back for his family's branding while I was chasing ships out in the Pacific. Also, the officer who'd been with my father in prison whom I had met on my mission, would be there. It would be interesting to connect with him once again. Finally, I had to formulate a plan to assume the training program in the six months between now and then.

During the next two weeks, I became friends with the Sikorsky HRS-2 helicopter trainer. Together we figured out it was about time I learned to fly helicopters. So in our downtimes, which were many hours this time of year, he began teaching me from the beginning the basics of flying a helicopter. I had my first simulator experience just before my weekend at home. It was a two-hour experience which I really enjoyed. I would finish up my 60 hours in the simulator after I returned. I could hardly wait to experience the real thing when it came time.

One evening out of the blue, my father called. He was very late arriving from his flight and was staying overnight before returning home. We spent over an hour talking to each other. It was the most extended and private conversation I'd had with him in many years. He commented that he'd had breakfast with Jim in Manila while on layover. After I mentioned that I had made reservations for the branding weekend, he replied, "Great! Jim mentioned that he was planning on being there when we had breakfast together. He wasn't sure about you, since he hadn't talked with you for a while." I could see my father smiling on the other end.

Betsy and Greg had set a date for their wedding in the base chapel. Both of them felt a military style wedding would be simple and not expensive. Greg wore his dress blues, and so did Betsy. He had one of his law partners as best man, and Betsy had me and her sister as maids of honor. It was a beautiful wedding overlooking Puget Sound. Their parents and many of their mutual friends were in attendance.

I called home a few days prior to Jim and I flying over for the branding. My father warned me that I might be surprised when we arrived. He also asked me if I mind flying our airplane back to the ranch. It was in Great Falls for its annual, and he would call to see if it was ready. I drove down to Jim's home the evening before leaving for Montana. Jim would be flying as an extra crew member, and I had a reservation on the flight. My father had called him earlier, letting him know the aircraft was ready.

It was another one of those beautiful, straightforward flights out of Seattle: Mount Rainier and Mount Adams on the right, and Mount Baker and Glacier Peak on the left. I was sitting in the center seat, looking past a gentleman sitting in the window seat. Yes, I was jealous of Jim sitting up in the cockpit, getting a bird's eye view of the surrounding terrain. Then the gentleman pulled down the shade so he could read his book. After that, I just let my seat back somewhat and let my mind wander over the next few days at home.

At Spokane, the gentleman deplaned, making everyone in the row stand up and let him out. Before the flight started to re-board, one of the flight attendants stopped and asked me to bring my bags and follow her. "Sorry, we just found out that you are Larry Becker's daughter and Jim's girlfriend." I just smiled at her and replied with a very gracious, "Thank you."

The flight attendant sat down beside me during the takeoff out of Spokane and introduced herself. "You do realize you are making every flight attendant a little bit jealous, don't you?"

"How do you mean?" I asked her.

"That guy up front is very much in love with you."

"How do you know that?" I asked her.

"Well, one reason is he hasn't screwed around since he met you. He is like your father on crew layovers. Of course, we all go out together for most meals, but that is where it ends for those two. Perfect gentlemen."

I acknowledged her remark and thanked her again for the upgrade. "That guy sitting in the window back there closed the shade so I could not see the mountains." We both laughed as the flight attendant returned to her duties before landing in Great Falls.

Landing in Great Falls, we proceeded to the telephone bank and called the aviation company. Ten minutes later, we were on our way to pick up my family's airplane. Jim did the pre-flight while I signed off on the work order at the aviation company office. Less than 15 minutes later, we were rolling down the runway and lifting off towards the ranch—it felt good flying my family's airplane again.

27

IT'S A PARTY

"Holy man!" Jim let out a cry, "Look at that crowd down there," as we made a pass over the ranch's home place.

"My dad informed me that I was in for a surprise, and it looks like a party." There were people, horses, motor homes, horse trailers, and tents everywhere. I was surprised the runway looked clear for us to land. It looked like there was action going on in the arena with dust flying everywhere. They even had a couple of grandstands around the arena. There was a play area not far away active with children. We taxied over to the hangar after landing and shut the aircraft down. It was going to be one wild weekend; neither of us knew if we really wanted to get out and join the crowd!

Our parents were both standing there when we opened the doors of the aircraft. There were hugs, handshakes, and kisses all around. We stood there in shock and wondered how many people were at the party. We passed a barbecue pit on the way to the house. Judy was busy making a potato salad large enough to feed an army.

A band was setting up near the arena. Someone mentioned that some people from California were filming the event. My father informed us that when the band started playing, the family would leave to gather cattle and bring them into the smaller pasture near the corrals. Jim's folks had brought three horses with them, and my parents were bringing along enough horses for the rest of the family.

Dinner was pot luck, and at the tables, everyone had a seat. My father made a little welcoming message for everyone that had come, hoping that they all were having fun. D.D. said a few words, and the whole family settled down to one great meal which was supervised by Mark's fiancée and her parents, who had made one more summer trip out to be with her.

The Air Force officer whom I met in Shemya while chasing drug traffickers across the Pacific on my return from the Middle East joined us. When I first met him that night in the mess hall, he looked tired and mentally exhausted. However, today it looked like he had a new lease on life. My father had said that D.D. had introduced him to one of her friends, so maybe that is one reason why he looked so much better this evening.

Many of the group followed us up to the summer pasture with their horses and trailers. The Sawtooth Ridge began to show in the distance the closer we traveled. When we started the roundup, the sun was topping the ridge. It was exhilarating to be out with the family again and Jim was with me, making it even better. Our grandparents were gone now, and both Mark and I missed them. Shortly after our father moved us to this ranch, our grandparents followed us and spent most of the time with us until we started school. I still felt that mother and my grandparents were watching over us. Branding and harvesting was one of our grandparents' favorite times while on the ranch. They treated

D.D. as a daughter when she became our stepmother—memories of earlier times.

Returning home, the party was still going. For us, it was going to be an early morning tomorrow, but Mark and I, along with our dates, joined the party. Our parents disappeared for the evening. Mark thought he saw them down by the creek with Mike, the Air Force officer, and his new friend. According to Mark, since Mike had arrived at the ranch over a week ago, my father and he had been spending a lot of time together, and it seemed to be for a reason. The first few nights it had been just the two men, but now the women were joining them.

It was very late when the band informed the crowd they would call it a night. About the same time, both couples returned from the creek and joined the partygoers for the last few dances.

Our parents dancing together always gave me a special feeling. They cared for each other very much. They set an excellent example for us kids and the rest of the world as they dealt with their daily lives. Tonight they were dancing the last dance just like they had so many times before.

The following day began before sunrise. The chores were completed around home before leaving for the corrals and branding. Now that we had our veterinarians in the family, both Mark and Judy and a couple of other visitors did the vaccinations and other medical chores. Jim and I did the wrestling after the calves came to the fire. Everyone else joined in and helped wherever possible. The whole process went almost like clockwork for the first time Mark and I could remember.

Early in the afternoon, branding was completed. Mike and our father went to the large pasture gate and opened it so that the calves could join their mothers.

Jim and I were standing with an arm around each other. Then something unique happened when the group of visitors surrounded us. Jim's father looked at his son and firmly said that Jim had something to say and he'd better get it done. Jim released his arm around me and turned towards me on his knees. Slowly he started on a little speech that he had memorized, pulling a soft little case out of his pocket, which looked like it had been through hell, out of his pocket. He reached for my left hand. "I know we both still have a lot of life to live before we tie the knot, but I love you with my whole heart, and I am asking you to marry me." He was putting the engagement ring on my left finger as he was making the request.

I looked at him and ordered him to stand up. Then I put both my hands around him and yelled, "Yes!"

That evening we were sitting on the deck overlooking the hay fields as the sun was setting on the Rockies. Listening to my father once again playing the piano, it seemed so quiet and peaceful. Jim finally spoke up, as others sat there enjoying their quiet time for the first time in days. "There was a time a few months back when I wondered if I would ever experience a night like this. We just happened to get shot down, and the two of us had to bail out. Fortunately, we landed close to one another. Far off in the distance, we could see lights speeding towards us. Our rescue people said it would be twenty minutes before they would get arrive.

"I was thinking of one person as those lights on the ground were zeroing in on us with no place to hide in the middle of the desert. It was about your father and how he felt that night in Nam—wondering if I would ever get the chance to ask you to marry me. I gave the choppers our GPS and gave them the approximate position of the enemy closing in on us. The next thing I remember was a voice coming on saying.

'Hit the fucking deck, mister. There is an incoming missile on its way.' I thought the voice sounded familiar, but I was yelling at my partner to hit the deck. That whole convey blew up not more than a couple thousand feet from us."

Quietly, almost beneath my breath, I said. "That was our incoming missile coming to save you. We thought we recognized your voice but weren't sure. We were maybe 40 miles away and could hear the anxious tone in your voice. So we decided to let one go to save you." Jim just smiled and pulled me closer as D.D. and the rest of the group sitting there smiled along with him and sat back in their seats, letting Larry continue playing the piano inside.

Then it was my turn. "Did everyone know about this except me?"

I didn't notice that the piano had stopped playing as my father appeared at the door. "Yup!" he said as he turned around, returned to the house, and sat back down at the piano. Everyone began to laugh. My face turned a bright red.

D.D. continued, "Your fiancéé stopped by back in May to ask our permission to marry you. We gave our permission, but your dad warned him it was going to be a tough next few years with you in the Navy."

Jim looked at me and commented, "I reminded your father that if we got married, you could travel on my passes since you wouldn't eligible for his anymore."

28

LIFE AFTER THE PARTY

The following day, everyone started leaving after the breakfast that Jim's father and I cooked with fresh rainbow trout, pancakes and scrambled eggs. Mark and Judy flew Jim and me to Great Falls to catch our flight for Seattle. They took the liberty to fly over their new home in the Sun River Valley along a major highway. This is where they planned to hang their shingle announcing a veterinary clinic.

Word travels fast among these small communities. Their business was starting to pick up even without the shingle. Judy's father had helped to outfit a couple of pickups with veterinary supplies so they could do farm visits. Furthermore, her mother had spent a significant part of the summer developing a computer program for the business and ensuring that all the proper licenses were in order.

Mark requested permission to land in Great Falls. The tower gave permission, as well as wind, weather and runway information to use in landing. Then the tower person joked, "I bet your parents are in that back seat making out again!"

We all laughed, and Mark remarked, "We left them at home in bed. My sister is sitting back there making out with her fiancéé today." Again, we all laughed as we began the approach to the airport. Mark was watching out for that famed crosswind that never went away.

Mark called the charter operations office requesting a car to take Jim and me over to the passenger terminal to check in and catch our flight. I had my full fare confirmed ticket and Jim had his employee pass. Seeing the ring on my finger, one of the agents said, "I see Jim finally is making you an honest woman."

They all laughed as I came back, "You mean, I am taking him off the market and making him an honest man, don't you?" The agents at the counter just laughed and put both of us in wide-open first class seats.

The sun was starting to set along the Cascades and over Puget Sound when we landed in Seattle. Then we went through the terminal and found our way to the employee parking lot to find Jim's car. There was a major league baseball game in Seattle tonight, so the going through Seattle was slow. I called in and let the base operations know that I would be in at 1300 the following afternoon. We sat on Jim's deck sipping a Kool-Aid. We'd had lunch in Great Falls while waiting for the flight. Not too far in the distance was Mount Pilchuck, with Glacier Peak standing tall at over 10,000 feet behind it. There was a lovely little meadow below the home with a couple of deer and some little rabbits running around.

"What's on your mind, my beautiful lady?" Jim asked.

"So many things that I can't tell which are more important. There is that Air Force officer I met while chasing ships across the Pacific. His name is Mike, and he is planning on retiring after spending a few weeks with dad. There's that lady my mother introduced him to while he was at the ranch. I am wondering how my parents are making it with help coming and going. Then there are Mark and Judy, and even though they've been together for a few years, they still haven't set a date to get married. The most important one is you and me. You do realize I could be sent back overseas anytime in the next few years, don't you?"

He gave me that killer smile of his, and very matter of fact answered, "I could be based out of New York next year or even Hawaii for that matter. We have just spent ten months apart, and it did not get in the way of our relationship, did it?"

I responded, "Being on an aircraft carrier out in the middle of some ocean isn't like flying some commercial aircraft with a group of good-looking women on board. Most pilots can have their choice anytime they want."

It was his turn now. "I not only have a great-looking woman back home, but I have a smart one that can out fish me. Most of those women would scream at a worm on a fishing hook. They don't know how to fly an airplane, much less find their way home. I am pleased with the one that I asked to marry me. Your dad and I are good friends, and our families are old Montana people. We believe in hard work, loving families, and being the best we can."

The following day after Jim cooked breakfast, I made my way back to Whidbey. Betsy was at the apartment starting to pack her belongings. Her commute was going to be somewhat longer than before, but being married made up for that. Her husband was also there carrying boxes and miscellaneous items out to the moving truck they had rented. I had decided to keep the apartment since it was so convenient to the base and the rent wasn't that bad. However, I would miss spending downtime with Betsy since she had become a great friend.

I returned to the training building by early afternoon, trying to catch up. Training and working were on my mind; so was the past weekend and the thoughts of home and especially Jim. The copter trainer yelled in from the other room, asking me if I wanted to go along on a rescue in the Cascades on Mount Rainier. A hiker had fallen in a crevasse and broken his leg. Fort Lewis had no rescue helicopters available, but Whidbey had one, although short one crew member.

That was until the training officer remembered seeing me in the office, and recalling his confidence in training me the last month, figured I could fill the position for a short time. "You have your fight suit on and we have an extra helmet." It did not take a second request to race out the door to the already running helicopter on the pad. Sitting in the right seat, I found the checklist and started to read off the checkmarks as the pilot answered each one with an affirmative, "Check."

We lifted off and set our responder for Mount Rainier. "Let us see what you learned in the simulator, mister." He motioned me to take control of the aircraft as we made our way towards the mountain. A call came in that two people would be picked up and delivered to a hospital in Seattle. One was in serious condition and the other in critical condition.

Meanwhile, the medical crew, including a doctor, was listening in on the conversation. The doctor interrupted to ask the victims' circumstances. He also asked about age and sex. The female had a brace on her leg, but the male sounded like he'd had a heart attack. They were doing CPR on him, and he was showing some pulse.

The crew in the back of the copter and the one below them were busy setting up the equipment they would need upon arrival in the area. Unfortunately, there was no stable place to land, so that the rescue would use the hoist and stretcher for both individuals. One crew member would be lowered down with the stretcher. When they arrived over the area, the pilot took control of the chopper and instructed me to start reading him the altitude as he lowered into position.

Both pilots were also in contact with the rescue crew in the back. It became the responsibility of the chief petty officer of the rescue team to lead the mission just below them. The pilot at the controls followed his directions. Looking out my window, I could see the stretcher with one crewman being lowered. Heart monitors and oxygen were attached to the patient as he came onboard. I could see the doctor and paramedic franticly working on him. Finally, the patient with the broken leg came on board resting the best as she could, worried about her partner.

The chief petty officer released his control of the aircraft and closed the door. "Let us get these people to the hospital as soon as possible." The lead pilot turned the power over to me as we proceeded to Seattle. I could feel the rush of adrenaline through my body as we set our sights on Seattle, some 90 miles away. We notified the civilian air traffic control that we had a couple of patients on board and wanted the airways cleared so as not to deviate from our mission. I felt comfortable flying the aircraft and keeping my mind off the cargo we were carrying.

I was able to see Seattle in the distance and the hospital at the same time. The number one leader called ahead to the hospital operations for permission to land. All of this time, I could hear the doctor onboard updating the hospital on the patient the crew was caring for. We came in over the freeway, and seeing the landing pad, I set the helicopter down very easy. Number one leader motioned to me not to shut down, just back off and let the chopper idle for a couple of minutes. The medical crew transferred the patients to hospital stretchers. Our crew doctor took a minute to pass some information on to the hospital personnel. Then he climbed back on board. "Mister, let us go home," the leader yelled and I slowly gave the chopper power and released the brakes. Up over the freeway and north to Whidbey.

"A beautiful afternoon for a pleasure flight to Mount Rainier, wouldn't you say, mister?" As the aircraft's leader was busy recording the mission in the records for later use, I looked over at him and smiled. I was too busy flying the aircraft to worry about small talk. He'd let me fly the majority of the time except for doing the maneuvering on the mountain. I was only too glad to have let him do that part.

It was quiet on the rest of the flight to Whidbey. The crew that had handled the rescue was storing all the equipment while we made our way to the base. I looked back once to see the doctor working on his report. The landing was smooth and easy. Everyone completed their respective responsibilities and the paperwork was completed.

I returned to my office in the training center. Unfortunately, I was now three days behind in my paperwork. It was a couple of hours later when the copter lead pilot requested a few minutes with me. He entered the office and sat across the table from me. Slowly he began to speak, "Mister, when I heard that the commander had appointed you to assume control here after David left, I felt not only left out, since I have more time then you, but I also thought I was more qualified.

"I felt you were just another Prowler pilot and didn't understand this whole operation. I even went to the commanding officer to make my point. Well, I must say he made the point that you were the most qualified person for the job. I informed him that you were not a helicopter pilot and are still new on the Prowler. Do you know what his comment was?"

I replied, "No."

"He bet me a hundred dollars that you would be flying the helicopter in less than a month."

I gave him a strange look, then asked, "Did you lose a hundred dollars today?"

"Yes." The chopper leader answered." Then with a smile, he made one last comment. "When I turned the controls over to you, I never thought in a million years you would take them. The commander was right when he promoted you. You are a damn good pilot."

Then he looked at my left finger. "You are engaged to be married?" I nodded my head yes. "Lucky guy."

It was a great day as I dug into my long overdue paperwork, wondering about the people I'd left off at the hospital. I was glad to be stationed in Washington with the mountains and the water. I could not wait to show Jim how to shuck and fry oysters.

A few hours later that evening, the same officer appeared back at the door. "Excuse me, but you are staying a little late, aren't you?"

"Just trying to catch up on my workload," I said.

He came back, "Do you like salmon with a baked potato and a salad?"

"Sounds good to me," I replied.

"I am going down to the mess for my meal, I'll bring you back a meal, and I can join you."

"Sounds good to me," I said returning to work, not even thinking about it. Fifteen minutes later, he entered my office carrying a dinner plate with salmon, potato, a salad, and bottled water. "What, no wine tonight?" I kidded him as he set the dinner down in front of me.

My mind told me to keep working; my stomach told me to back off and enjoy the meal. The officer started conversing with me. "When you first arrived here on base and began flying the Prowler, every single officer wanted to ask you out. One finally did, and you very plainly informed him that you didn't date officers. Then you showed up at the New Year's Eve ball with one. What changed your mind on dating an officer." Long story short, if possible!" I almost broke out laughing.

I tried to explain with as short of a story as possible. "My fiancé had convinced a ticket agent that he had to sit next to me on a two hour flight home for Christmas. He was traveling as a company employee on standby, and I was a full fare passenger. He mentioned that he wasn't working on New Year's Eve and wondered if the Navy had some kind of dance. I said yes, and he asked me if I would like an escort. Since I didn't have one, and he was a civilian and might enjoy it, I said yes. I asked my father about him since he also flies for the same airline. His only comment was that he was a nice guy.

"We talked a couple of times on the phone after I returned from my parents' home in Montana. He seemed like a nice guy for a civilian, then of course, he was a good-looking commercial pilot. When I kind of kiddingly teased him about being a pilot and all of those flight attendants, he just laughed it off. New Year's Eve, he shows up in a Naval officer uniform and I just about had a kitten."

We both laughed at my story. "Until this summer, he and my father used to fly together. Now my father is flying out of Detroit to Asia and hates the commute from Montana to Detroit.

"What does your father fly?" he asked.

"He is now flying the new 747/400, and he enjoys it," I answered back.

We continued to talk for a while. He was married to a nurse; together, they had two children. He had just returned from Middle East duty after being gone for over a year. He was happy that he could slip into this teaching position where staying home longer might be one of the perks. Our conversation lasted for another hour when he decided he better get home. I looked at my watch and made the same decision hoping to hear from Jim sometime tonight.

The apartment was dark except for a small light I had left on earlier. It had been a very long but rewarding day. My thoughts were still with the couple that we had left at the hospital earlier today. According to the doctor on board, they were husband and wife, and the outdoors was their passion. Hopefully everyone would be all right, and they would be back climbing mountains sooner rather than later. I noticed that Jim had left a message on my recorder saying he was leaving on a trip tomorrow afternoon, so I felt I needed to call him.

New trainees started arriving in September and Prowler, helicopter, P-3C and weapons officer training were in full swing. The helicopter leader and I started working together as a team. My three week leave was coming up, and I felt comfortable leaving with him in charge. October was always another family time on the ranch when everyone gathered to help out. This year, Jim's parents and mine were doing their end of summer duties a week apart.

29

HOME FOR FALL RANCH DUTIES

We decided to drive back to Montana early this year so we could spend some quiet time together. It would be 13 hours of just being together without interruptions or the outside world getting in our way.

This time Jim drove up to my apartment the evening before departing for Montana. It was dinner out at our favorite restaurant. The following day we took a different route to Montana, traveling over Stevens Pass. Neither of us had ever crossed this way before. We noticed the fall colors along the way. When we reached Leavenworth, Washington, with its Bavarian style, we felt it was worthy of an overnight stay. To try out some of the great food and wines it had to offer, we found a nice Bavarian style hotel in the central part of the town. We parked the car and started exploring the quaint little village, having dinner in an outdoor restaurant and enjoying the comings and goings of other visitors to the area. Exploring various other attractions placed around the village was an experience in itself. "We are going to have to return when they have the Christmas lighting everyone is talking about," Jim commented.

We crossed Washington State the following day as the sun was rising. That evening we spent at the Lake Coeur d'Alene Resort Golf Course in Idaho. We checked in early enough to play nine holes of golf—it was my first time playing the game. Following that, a romantic dinner by the lake on the deck, with some soft music playing in the background, made for a beautiful evening. We had spent almost ten months apart during Desert Storm without losing the feeling between us. Jim knew, just like my father did, that he could be activated anytime. I knew that life in the Navy was changing for women. In the future and even now in the Middle East, women were increasingly in combat zones alongside men.

The following day we were on our way again, stopping in Missoula for lunch and finally arriving in Augusta. I wanted to pause at the high school and see if anyone I remembered was still there. It had been ten years since I had graduated. The class had only seven students; we were all friends. It looked like the football team was on the field practicing, so the school must be open.

We walked into the front entrance to find the principal still in his office talking to an adult. He saw me through the hallway window and motioned to us to enter. I introduced him to Jim. Then he introduced us to the new teacher. "This is one of our prize students," he said to the new teacher. "Augusta graduate, Annapolis graduate, and a pilot for the U.S. Navy. We turn out only the best here in Augusta. I'm proud not only of the school but the students too." I was embarrassed as I acknowledged the teacher.

We left his office and started to explore the school and the graduates pictures alone the hallways. There were a couple of basketballs sitting on the gym floor. I picked one up and threw it from the 3 point line, easily dropping it through the basket.

"Whoa! Let us see how good I am with that ball." Jim picked up the ball and shot it from the same 3 point line. It bounced a couple of times on the rim and dropped to the floor. I stood there trying not to laugh.

A voice from the back of the gym called out, "She still has it!" Then the coach smiled and came over and hugged me. "Welcome back, young lady!" This left Jim to try that basket one more time. This time it bounced once on the rim and went in. Looking around, he found no one was paying any attention to him.

We pulled into the ranch as the sun was setting over the Rockies with a cold breeze coming off of them. This time it was piano and guitar together playing beautiful music from inside the house. Jim whispered to me, "Let us sit out here on the deck and listen." We sat down on one of the porch swings. He opened the cooler, and poured a glass of wine for each of us. We toasted each other with the music coming from inside the house. "What a way to come home," I said.

The music stopped, then a voice from inside the house said, "I wonder where those kids are?" My father was surprised as he opened the door and found us sound asleep on the swing, with a couple of empty wine glasses sitting on the floor.

D.D. put together a fast, simple dinner while her husband woke the couple up. "Why didn't you just come in instead of waiting out here for us to quit?" asked my father.

Jim was the first to speak up, "It was so beautiful; we didn't want to disturb you. Besides, listening to you guys playing, and watching the sunset was what we needed. By the way, I didn't know D.D. played the guitar. You guys together make great music."

D.D. responded, "We always figure it is better than fighting even though making up afterward is a lot of fun." They all laughed as D.D. set the table with leftover casserole. I always was amazed at my parents' marriage. It was so different from some of my friends who always complained about their parents fighting all. They both had been through traumatic experiences in their previous lives: D.D. with her first marriage and my father with his time as a POW.

The next morning, we awoke to the odor of breakfast coming through the door. Judy and D.D. were in the kitchen while Mark and my father were out getting the stock ready for the day. The sun had not even come up over the plateau yet. Mark and Judy had brought one of their veterinary vans with supplies to cover all the doctoring needs for the day.

It would be another busy fall day in The Shadows of Sawtooth Ridge. First we would round up the cattle on some five thousand acres of open range, separating the calves from their mothers and then doctoring and pregnancy testing the mother cows. While this was in progress, D.D. was working with the two cattle buyers, cutting out some of the weaker calves and preparing the rest for shipping. Four semis arrived early to transport the calves. Jim's parents and mine decided to start loading them up while the others kept doctoring the cattle.

Mark, Judy and Judy's father traded off with each other doing the pregnancy testing. Judy's father, a retired veterinarian from Oregon, was a welcome sight for both of them today. He had come out earlier to help the new vets with the usual fall veterinarian duties. Their practice was almost needing three vets this time of year.

The last cow went through by late afternoon. Jim and I helped my brother and his fianceé pick up all the needles and empty medicine bottles. I could not believe my brother and especially his wife: both had manure on their bodies from head to toe and acted like it was just another day at work. My little brother had come of age and his fiancéé was equal with him. Three large casseroles were waiting for us in the small barn that sat beside the corrals. Mark and Judy joined us after they cleaned up. Everyone laughed as they entered the barn looking just like any other ranching couple.

D.D. and I were returning to the summer pasture after taking a load of replacement calves to the home place. We could see two guys braving the wind as they finished loading the final semi. They were Jim and my father having a hard time keeping their hats on, and again wearing jackets they had worn earlier in the day. D.D. and I mentioned to each other how close these guys were when working together. Everyone else was gone except them and the range rider. We went over to help them finish loading. Finally, after the last truck was loaded and gone, we loaded the horses in the trailer and returned to the ranch, leaving the range rider and his wife behind in their isolated home.

There were still chores to be done at the home place: Putting the horses away, milking the two cows, and feeding the calves that D.D. and I had brought home earlier. Jim always wondered how my father could always stay so slim and in shape. Now he knew why, because the guy never slowed down. I told him that D.D. was the same way, as she always worked out in the hotel gym, or they would go out for runs when they drove home together from Texas. My mother would often ride her horses or run a regular five mile route when she was home. Like my father, D.D. had another profession besides raising a family. She wrote a couple newspaper articles a week. Then having 2-3 books a year published.

Jim's family was somewhat different. His mother was a teacher and his father pretty much stuck to running the ranch. When the children were older his parents would take a vacation once a year by themselves. His brother and sisters were always brilliant. They all graduated at the top of their classes. He had done the same, and all the children went on scholarships when it came to college. His family was surprised that he decided to take flying lessons at 16 and ROTC came next in college. When he graduated and went into the Navy, they were even more surprised. He was the only military member of the family. His father had assumed the ranch from his father and had become exempt from the military during the Vietnam era.

The following day Jim and I left for his parents' place in Roundup. We took four horses and drove Dakota's pickup with horse trailer and living quarters attached. My parents would follow later when the range rider came down to do the chores and stay at the house. Suddenly, it became quiet around the home place, except that the calves still made their presence known with their consent mooing.

That evening Jim's parents and his two sisters prepared a large meal for all of us. Early the following day before sunrise, the riders left the home place and made their way to the pasture. It was late afternoon before all the cattle were rounded up and moved closer to the home, where there were corrals to work the cattle.

The following day the whole process that had just happened at our ranch was now happening at the Evanston's ranch. The only difference was that only one vet was doing the hard work. The action only halted at noon for a meal. The semis started arriving in the late afternoon shortly after Jim's brother and father had finished picking out the replacement heifers and a few steers for their family's meat supply for next year.

When the excitement slowed down, the women were left sitting on that front porch watching the men finish up the chores. Jim's sister asked a big question of me: "When are you two getting married?"

"Right now, we both are too busy to even think about it," I replied. I still have five more years of commitment time with the Navy. Both of us want to take one day at a time. When the time comes, we will let everyone know."

Then Jim's mother entered into the conversation. "These days, with both males and females working to further their careers, it is hard to make good decisions. But we all know that both of you belong together. We have never seen Jim happier than he is now. He missed you while you both were in the Gulf. He mentioned a couple of weeks ago that it was your team that saved him from being captured." I smiled and just felt lucky we were there at the right time. I would have hated to see Jim end up like my father.

We stayed with Jim's parents for a couple of days before returning to my parents' home. My parents wanted to have their horses back and our help on the fall cattle drive from the summer pasture to home. But unfortunately, it seemed like it took us forever to return to Great Falls, with the wind blowing directly at us most of the way. It was late afternoon when we finally entered my parents' home place.

It was early the following day and the sky was clouding over when we started up the road to the summer pasture. The morning temperature was sitting near freezing. The eastern slopes of the Rockies were going to hand us one miserable day. It looked like winter was now beginning in The Shadows of Sawtooth Ridge. Daylight was beginning to appear when the group started to gather the cattle. It was noon before the actual drive started. D.D. decided to drive the truck and trailer back to the home place before the cattle and riders began down the road. Everyone decided to forgo the noontime meal when the snow started to lightly fall. The wind turned to a northeastern direction quickly becoming stronger and colder.

The cattle kept wanting to turn their backs toward the wind, but the group kept pushing them forward. We were on top of a plateau with no place to protect ourselves and the cattle from the harsh wind and snow coming almost directly at us. Although somewhat covered, even my face seemed frozen.

Our canvas dusters shed some of the cold, but not all of it, and frost was building up on them. Even our horses were fighting it, trying to turn their backs toward the wind like the cattle. Visibility beyond a few hundred feet ahead was becoming an impossibility.

The sun was starting to set, when up towards the front of the herd, we could hear screaming, a car horn and yelling. The cattle began to turn and headed off the road. The wind was blowing the snow so hard that no one could see what made the cattle turn. My dad raced up alongside the herd, trying to turn them back and get them going straight. When the group finally was able to see what was causing all the commotion, it surprised all of us. A gate was open going into the pasture with the truck and horse trailer crossways and blocking the road. Judy and D.D. were the ones yelling like mad to get the cattle to turn into the pasture where they belonged. The group continued to follow the cattle through the gate and down to the home place.

D.D. and Judy closed the gate, and returned to the home place. They had the barn open as the riders came in. While the riders were in the tack room trying to warm up, Judy and D.D. removed the saddles, bushed each horse down and put a blanket on them. I don't remember the last time I was this cold.

Before they had finished up the last horse, I had joined them while my father was getting a couple of the hay bales for the mother cows. We ladies left the horse barn and made our way up to the house, leaving the men to finish the chores. D.D. and Judy had managed to keep the casserole warm since they hadn't had it for the noon meal. It was another hour before all the men descended on the house for a hot dinner. The late fall blizzard was still blowing from the northeast and snow mixed with freezing rain made it even more unbearable than usual. The patio and sidewalks were slick, and so was the ground in many places

It was finally time to settle down around the big rock fireplace and tell stories. It had been a long day. According to our father, D.D. and Judy had saved the day, otherwise we would still be looking for that gate to the pasture. So it was again family time in the shadows of the Sawtooths. Everyone was staying for the evening, but we were too tired for anything else. Mark and Judy had arrived mid-afternoon after attending to a couple of veterinary appointments. Both she and Mark decided to stay until morning since they figured Judy's parents, who had stayed over for a few weeks, could handle the chores at their home place.

My father settled down at his piano and started to play some of the most beautiful music I had heard in a long time. I must have fallen asleep in Jim's arms as he carried me off to bed. It wasn't too long until it was just D.D. and Larry sitting together by themselves at the piano making slow and easy romantic music.

The following day, as I awoke in Jim's arms, I slowly rolled over to him. I planted a kiss on his mouth as he began to wake up. Looking at me with a sexy smile, he made a comment that surprised even me.

"I just realized last night that I want a marriage like your parents. Two people with one soul and one heart."

I smiled as I cuddled close to him. "I remember my father and natural mother being sort of that way. Unfortunately, my father had to leave before they could put their marriage to a real test.

"Then there was D.D. and dad. I can never forget my father encouraging her to reach out independently and not depend on him. I remember him telling us that just because he and D.D. were married, didn't mean life stopped. I found out that she had her own life when we drove home together from Texas. People know her and love her. So many of them have helped her through the rough part of her life. Even when we walked into a couple of different restaurants in Albuquerque, waiters and chefs knew her and catered to her like a long lost friend coming home. She became my idol after that trip. Did you know that we even went up in a balloon in Albuquerque at sunrise with what seemed like a hundred other balloons?"

Jim just laid there listening to this beautiful woman be like her mother. He turned his head, looking at my brown eyes. "You are so much like her, with your father added in for smarts."

Finally, breakfast was ready, with everyone sitting at the big long dining room table as Mark and Judy served the breakfast. I had heard through Mark that he and Judy had had many ups and downs the last few years. Mark and our father had had quite a few discussions down on the old cottonwood stump over the years. I knew one of them was about Judy. D.D. really liked Judy and her parents. Once, she compared them to our mother's parents. They had come out from Oregon and helped with remodeling the house and setting up the practice. Since Judy's dad was a retired veterinarian, he had a good idea of setting one up.

It was finally time to return to Washington State and our professions. As we left the home place, we waved to my father near the wheat storage bins. There was two large semi's taking wheat on to be taken to Washington.

The snow that fell in the early fall blizzard yesterday had all but melted. This side of the Rockies always seemed to have wind, and today it was blowing as usual. We made another overnight stop in Leavenworth for dinner, with a relaxing evening by the hotel fireplace sipping a glass of wine. We made each other the promise to return for the Christmas tree lighting on the first of December.

In early afternoon we arrived at my apartment near Whidbey. We had a small lunch before Jim left for his home in Everett. It was sad seeing Jim go after having spent so much time together the past three weeks. But we both realized it was time to get back to the reality of our jobs.

30

NEW ORDERS

The next day I returned to my office to catch up on the workload. Paperwork was always the most boring job of the Navy. My commander walked into the office just about noon. "How was your leave, mister?" He asked.

"Busy!" I answered. "My parents never seemed to sleep. Especially this time of the year."

"I understand. Being from a ranching family in Oklahoma I've learned to stay away from mine this time of year." Both of us laughed. Then he became serious. "The group that you are training on the Prowler will be joining the 7th fleet in the Pacific on the carrier USS Nimitz in mid-January. Mister, you will be their squadron leader; it will be a change in plans. Any questions, mister?"

I just looked at him, dumbfounded for a few moments. I had received my promotion, but now it would be a much different position and challenge. "Yes, sir," I finally replied.

"What just happened?" I thought to myself, wondering how I would manage the next couple of months. Most of the new group had just been on for a few weeks, and now we had only two and one-half months to prepare for the next chapter. Thanksgiving and Christmas would mean time lost. Then I thought of my father and Jim, knowing that they worked for a 24/7 company. "Why not make this operation work the same way?" I thought to myself. It would be like that on the carrier when we arrived.

I set a briefing time and notified all of the leaders to be there, but before doing that, I called my commander to bless the plan. He offered to help me set it in motion. Thus, preparing for the first briefing, I had my assistant send out the first of many briefing times. The commander and I worked through the afternoon to prepare the department for a 24/7 workweek. Unfortunately, completion of the plan still left us missing some pieces. "Why don't we use the reserves to fill in the open spots and work around their schedules?" he asked. "Their schedules are in my office. We can make the adjustments first thing in the morning." I let out a sigh of relief, knowing it could work.

I always had some soft piano music playing in the background of my office since I began occupying it. The commander, relaxing in his chair, asked about the music. I replied, "That is my father playing the piano. My stepmother made a CD of it one evening and gave it to me."

"Wow! I never knew your father played the piano. Then, of course, even though I was his commander here at Whidbey, I never had a real conversation with him. He enjoyed working with the younger pilots when he was doing his reserve time. So many of them today call him Pops! Your fiancéé was one of his favorite works."

I was not even surprised. "Somehow, I figured that. They knew too much about each other before I came along."

"I will see you in the morning at 0800 over breakfast with your fill-in leaders. All right?" he asked.

I stood up and saluted him as he left my office. I was wondering at the same time why I qualified for so much help from so many people. It seemed like the whole squadron was at my service. I stopped by the mess and picked up dinner on the way home.

I hadn't called my parents yet, and had not even talked to Jim since returning to the base. Upon entering the apartment, the phone was ringing. It was Jim, and he seemed concerned since I had not answered my phone or called since returning from Montana. "Just very busy, honey.

Then I went into my news of the last couple of days. "When I leave on this assignment, you and I will be of the same rank." Jim was a Lieutenant Commander now and Joni would be the same.

"Wow! Did anything else happened that I can't control?"

I laughed and said, "Yes!"

I then filled him in on the whole week and why I hadn't called or even returned his call. "Oh by the way when you come up and do your reserve duty in the future. You will be helping train the new pilots."

After a long, drawn-out breath, he commented, "First, I am leaving on a 12 day trip tomorrow, which will give 12 days to think. Second, I do want a good-looking blonde that is smart enough to buy me dinner." They both laughed at that one. "Hey, I've got to call my parents since I haven't talked to them lately either." Both of us said our goodbyes and hung up.

Meanwhile, Jim was trying to relax and wondering what he had gotten himself into with this lady. There was no way she was going to be an ordinary farm wife. The kitchen was not her home, but the cockpit of an airplane was to her liking. He was proud of her, and it would take a lot of patience before they would be able to marry. Every day was a new surprise; he always looked forward to them. Now when he did his reserve duty, she was going to be his boss, but of equal rank. His reserve duty was going to be interesting.

Before the night was over, I made a long overdue call to my family back in Montana. My father answered the phone. At first he just listened to the news that I was telling him.

Then he filled me in a little on his life. D.D. was in New York with her agent discussing another book and another movie to be made for television. My father was flying to New York to work his overseas flight to Tokyo. D.D. would be joining him on this 12 day trip. Her father seemed excited for her to finally join him for the first time since he began flying out of the East Coast. Until now, she had always had commitments in other parts of the country.

His final comment was: "I've always been second in command and never first. So you are blazing your trail. Good luck."

I had always looked up to him as a leader. Now he was stepping aside to let me make up my own mind.

Next morning's 0800 briefing after mess came very quickly, and soon I was standing to brief my command on their mission for the next few months.

It would take teamwork on all of our parts to make it a success. It was an hour before I finished the briefing and gave out assignments for each unit. The personnel were standing at attention as I dismissed them. I heard some grumblings about a woman being in charge. Another one of the male voices spoke up. "I don't know if a woman commander is good or bad, but she is easy on the eyes." Unfortunately, they were about to find out how hard I could be on them. I noticed that there were a few women in the class of new pilots.

Each morning and evening we had a briefing. Jim was one of the reserve pilots that took turns in the training process over the next few months. Somehow the two of us managed to have dinner together when he was here. Otherwise, Jim was making two ten day trips with the airline each month. He mentioned that he saw my father and D.D. on one of his trips to Bangkok and had dinner with them.

It was all so inconceivable how people could get together halfway around the world: My father had managed to meet up with me a few times while I was in the Middle East and Jim mentioned to me that he might catch up with me while in my ports of call. Neither one of us discussed a time when we could get married. Life was moving along almost too fast for each of us.

Thanksgiving was the next interruption of the training. Both of our families managed to make it out to the coast for the holiday. Dinner was at Jim's home, and to my surprise, I found out that Jim could put on a lovely dinner for all of us. It was a wonderful four-day weekend for everyone.

He did not have to, but it seemed that Jim was on base working with new people every minute he was free from his regular job with the airlines. He led a team of three trainees on training missions to some interesting places. One of his favorite places was the Chinook Pass area of the Cascades. Another was the Yakima Training Center near Yakima, Washington. They also did a training mission in northern Montana. Any pilot who was having trouble would spend extra time in the simulator once they returned to base. All had carrier experience in their previous training. Still, one of the other trainers insisted that the entire group go through the whole program again.

During a week's leave at Christmas, both of us were able to have time off together for some R and R. The holiday gathering would be in Montana in the Shadows of Sawtooth Ridge. The men teamed up to make Christmas Eve dinner. Jim and I brought some salmon from

Seattle. My father provided the beef from the ranch. D.D., Jim's mother Bess, Judy, and her mother Laura all teamed up to make Christmas dinner.

Christmas dinner completed, everyone gathered around in the great room near the massive stone fireplace. It was here that Mark and Judy announced that they were to be married in June. They had decided on Pendleton, Oregon, near Judy's parents. Mark remarked, "Judy and I have been living together for almost three years. Both of our parents have been very influential in our decision. We care for each other very much, even though there have been ups and downs."

I thought out loud, not realizing what I was saying, "Wow! My little brother is going to beat me to the altar."

Jim looked over at me, again with that got you smile. "Mister, follow your dreams. I will be waiting until the time comes."

Both my father and D.D. smiled at us. Then D.D. spoke up first. "You never know what lies on the other side until you reach it. Your dad encouraged me to follow my heart and soul, even if we were married. I have loved being your mother, but I have also yearned for something else in my life. Whenever I told your father what I wanted to do, he was to the point with no argument and just said, 'Go chase your dreams, don't let me hold you up. We will work it all out in the end somehow,' and we have."

I knew these two had something special between them. My father had two independent women in the family who he encouraged to follow their own dreams, and he was proud of both of them. His son was marrying the girl of his dreams, and was also enjoying his chosen profession.

That evening Jim and I lay in bed staring up at the ceiling and listening to my father playing the piano. Tomorrow both of us would return to the coast. Jim had an international trip and I was still preparing for my squadron's first deployment.

31

OPERATION SOUTHERN WATCH

We were back in Washington State before New Year's Day this time. There would be no New Year's Eve ball. Jim was beginning a 12 day trip before the ball and would not return until mid-January.

February 3, the carrier left Bremerton, Washington. My squadron would be joining the ship two days later. Each of the four crew members on the Prowler knew their respective duties inside and out. Every scenario that could and would go wrong was worked out and checked inside and out. The aircraft ground crew were either bused or drove themselves to the aircraft carrier's port.

My fellow officers and I were briefed on our deployment. The USS Nimitz was to relieve the USS Kitty Hawk in the Arabian Gulf on February 21 to take its place as part of Operation Southern Watch. I would be returning to the Middle East again, only this time as a squadron leader and flying an aircraft I was beginning to love. Women were becoming more common in my chosen field as our restriction from combat zones was lifted. Three other women were in the squadron with me, and we were outperforming the men in many instances.

The morning of the 3rd, the squadron left Whidbey. No one had any idea when we would return to our home base. We were to meet the Nimitz out at sea as it made its way across the Pacific. Jim stood off the side in his flight suit, saluting me as I departed the ramp, made a turn, and proceeding towards the taxiway. We would be taking off two at a time, leaving Whidbey behind. There were six aircraft making their way to the carrier.

A couple of hours out, we met up with the aircraft carrier. Landing on an aircraft carrier would be a challenge this time with the weather. I requested permission to come aboard as the ship was moving through the rough winter seas. There was a storm brewing, moving in from Alaska. It seemed that the squadron had flown right into it. We made one pass around the carrier and set up in a pattern for landing. Being the leader, I went first. I lined up with the aircraft carrier, remembering my father's advice more than ever right now. He had said, "Catch the ship as it comes up in rough seas." I had also shared this advice with my squadron. With my hook down as I approached the carrier, it caught the first cable right away, stopping the aircraft.

My crew and I quickly exited the aircraft after parking. It was time to watch the other five of my squadron and see if their training made a difference. The last aircraft was the only one that missed the first cable, but it managed to catch the second one. My weapons officer patted me on the back as we watched the last one come to a complete stop. "Mister, your training paid off today. I hope we don't have to land again in this kind of weather."

The chief petty officer was standing beside me directing traffic and smiled. "Mister, this is going to be a wild ride for a few days until we exit this storm. You'd better find your quarters and sit tight for a wild ride."

My squadron met in the briefing room, where the ship's commander welcomed us. He briefed us on a few items to do and more not to do. One of the ship's officers showed us the mess location. Then he led the men to one sleeping quarter and the women to another. Even though we were separate, I liked the idea that we were still next to each other. There was a desk in each berth where I could do my homework for the morning briefings after breakfast. I was amazed that there was Wi-Fi on board so that I could contact family and, of course Jim, back home. Since he flew the circle route between Seattle and Asia. Which is the same route our aircraft carrier would be taking. He might check in once in awhile and see how we were proceeding.

We were the only Prowler squadron on board the carrier. There was also 2 squadrons of F-14A that had come aboard earlier. I was wondering when I would meet those two leaders.

My first night onboard ship was horrible as the ship tried to change paths due to the rough seas. There was one more rough night before the seas started to settle down somewhat. I finally went topside to see what daylight at sea looked like. Off in the distance, I could see two more ships escorting the carrier. One of the ship's officers asked if I would like a bridge tour since he was going that way. I did not hesitate to say, "Yes."

He led the way showing me the different communication and operation rooms on the way up. I had spent the summer of my junior year at Annapolis serving onboard a destroyer and knew some of the components of most ships. The bridge was a maze of instruments, computers and GPS systems, ensuring that we would stay out of trouble.

Once reaching the bridge and explaining in detail the workings of the carrier, the officer asked a question. "I've been wondering if your father's name is Larry Becker."

I gave him a strange look, thinking to myself that this officer is no older than I am, so he can't be a friend of my father. However, before I questioned him about why he was asking, I gave him an affirmative, "Yes."

He smiled, informing me that his father was in Vietnam with my father where they both were POWs. "I am an Annapolis graduate too. I was a few years ahead of you and remember you as a freshman. When your name appeared on the freshman roster, I always wondered if you were Larry's daughter. My father was on the same evacuation flight as yours. Mine came off just before yours. I remember your father crying, 'No!' when he hugged you and your grandparents. I will always remember you telling your father, 'Mommy said don't cry, daddy.' I will always remember that scene so many years ago."

"You remember that far back?" I asked, surprised that someone would remember that day. We then departed to our respective areas after promising to have dinner together the following evening.

I took a lesson from Betsy about a daily briefing. Each morning and evening, the crews would gather in the briefing room. Information and problem solving were the order of each briefing.

I would get together with Donny, the officer whose father was in prison with my father, many times in the next few months over dinner. He was married with two little girls, and showed off his photos of them and his wife. She was a grade school teacher, and because of moving so often, had taught in many different schools. His father left the Navy after Vietnam and finished law school. He was now a judge and planning on retiring very shortly.

The carrier entered the Arabian Gulf on March 18. On the 21st, it assumed its position as part of Operation Southern Watch. The United States military was to enforce the no-fly zone between the 32nd and 33rd parallels. Usually we flew missions with three aircraft at a time. The carrier force made several port calls during our tour. They were Mina Sulman, Bahrain, Dubai, UAE, Fujairah, UAE, and Khasab, Oman.

When not flying missions in the no-fly zone, set up by the United Nations to protect the Kurds from Iraq's government, my crew ate together, briefed together, read books, and watched movies in the entertainment room. Meals were great, but I yearned for a steak medium-rare.

My family had managed to tape most of Mark and Judy's wedding in June and forwarded me the video. One free evening, much of my team and I were seated in the briefing room watching the wedding take place. My father and stepmother played some of the couple's chosen music during the ceremony. It was fun watching the fathers welcome Mark and Judy to the respective families. Judy's parents had been so helpful to the couple while they were setting up their veterinary practice. In addition, her father had an eye for carpentry work and could build or remodel anything.

Women had to adhere to the customs of the various Middle Eastern countries they visited when making port calls. A few of them complained but willingly observed the customs. Most days, the onboard ship time was 12 to 18 hours in intense heat. Finally, in July, Joni's Prowler squadron was ordered to destroy all radar stations. They were left behind when the Iraq left the area. The mission was a success and was the squadron's last hurrah before returning to the United States.

The carrier would be returning to Bremerton and the air squadrons to Whidbey.

Returning home, we stopped at Singapore to take some well-deserved free time. Standing on the docks when we put into port was Jim, with a great big smile on his face. When I had talked with him just a couple of days prior, he did not indicate that he would meet me along the way. It was two full days of bliss before he had to return to Tokyo. We had a beautiful dinner overlooking the city and waterfront. Early the following day, he was gone, leaving me alone in the room. I had to laughed at Jim's cell phone alarm as it went off singing, "I'm leaving on a jet plane." It was mid-day as I returned to the carrier after a welcome rest. The whole evening felt like a dream. It was the last port of call for the aircraft carrier.

The seas after Japan again became rougher, and the squadron made a couple more surveillance missions along the way to keep eyes on other forces in the area so as not to interfere with the carrier force movements. The Prowler squadron returned to Whidbey, two days before the carrier task force docked at its homeport of Bremerton. Standing there as my team parked our aircraft, was Jim again, in his flight suit. Many times I wondered why I deserved such a good-looking, funny and intelligent guy. Today I just smiled at him after I parked the aircraft. Patiently he waited for me to complete the aircraft check and the paperwork.

I returned home safely and he thought as beautiful as ever. Although he was a civilian, he could be activated anytime for active duty. I still had a couple of more years to serve before I could even think of another field. He was happy for me becoming a success in my chosen profession. There were so many men he knew who had wives at home tending the fires while they worked. I would not be one of them. Some of those same men were now getting divorced because the wives found out they were missing something outside the home.

Sometimes I wondered how come I deserved a guy like him. He was always interested in my goals and achievements. This guy has got to have every flight attendant in the airline chasing him. Although her father never said much about him, she came to realize that he respected Jim and treated him like a son. Very professionally, I walked over to him, standing there with a dozen roses in his hands. Then I walked up to him and we traded salutes with each other. He then handed me the roses and asked, "Is that all I get with a dozen roses?" I laughed, giving him the biggest hug and kiss yet.

32

THE SQUADRON RETURNS

We stopped at my empty apartment and changed into some comfortable clothes. I knew where I wanted to spend the first half of the day home. We went to the beach, stopping along the way to pick up a bucket, rake and shovel. The tide was low when we reached the shore. I started searching for oysters, showing Jim how it was done. He was wondering how a cowgirl from Montana knew so much about shucking oysters on the shores of Puget Sound. Once we had our limit, we found a washed up log and sat down together to gather our thoughts. "Why don't we get married?" I blurted out, surprising even myself.

He gave me a long look and asked, "Do you mean it?"

"Yes!" I replied, "Before I change my mind."

"Alright, now that we've decided to get married, do you have any ideas where and when?"

"I've had six months to think about it, but I have to make a few phone calls before its final."

"Wow! You meet your favorite girl on the Navy tarmac for only the second time in 6 months and she already has our wedding figured out. Nothing surprises me more than you do, Joni."

Over an open fire pit, we barbecued oysters and drank wine. We discussed the next couple of months. It was August, and both of us wanted an early fall wedding. Jim was quite concerned that I would not continue with my dreams. He was not going to stand in the way of my vision. But on the other hand, he was in love with me enough to let me follow those dreams without him if need be.

He had been around many men who did not let their wives dream. It was one of the reasons he had stayed single for so long. His parents had an equal marriage where they followed their dreams and still managed to make a great home for Jim, his brother and sisters. When he first started flying with my father, he found out that Larry felt the same way. Deep down my father felt terrible that my birth mother, Eve, had to stay home and take care of the children while he was away for four years. As a result, she never had a chance to follow her dreams.

Now my father was married to D.D., and Jim knew how well my father had supported her dreams. They had worked out the logistics, so that even while raising Mark and me, they were always together, celebrating each other's achievements. Jim wanted to make sure that married life for us meant that continuing our dreams was a goal of both of us. Together we seemed assured it could work. We were in love and honest with each other.

I finally made the call home to let my parents know what our plans were. My father answered and I asked him if D.D. could pick up the other phone. She was in the office working on another story, and when she picked up the phone, I announced our marriage. After that, both men just listened in on the conversation. It was over an hour later when we stopped talking. Back in Montana, it was midnight. We had decided on no church wedding and no wedding inside of a hall, but instead a barn wedding. There were to be no uniforms, no wedding dress, and no tuxes— just two people dressed in their everyday clothes. We both were from Montana and I wanted just a Montana wedding. D.D. would see if they could do it the last of September, then she would let me know.

I hung up the phone and turned around to find no Jim. I searched the whole apartment, finally finding him in bed sound asleep. He had mentioned to me that he had an early mission in the morning before we had even started the evening. He looked so comfortable sleeping soundly with a smile on his face. I removed my clothes and climbed into bed, putting my arm around him. "Yes!" I did love him and had missed him the last six months. Even though we had one night in Singapore, it wasn't the same as being home in my bed. When I finally saw some sunlight showing through the window in the early morning, Jim had already departed, leaving a note on the mirror in the bathroom. The note stated, "Dinner tonight at our favorite restaurant at 7 PM. I am buying." I had the day off, so it was time to contemplate the next couple of months.

I had decided I wanted to get married. Jim was the guy I wanted to be with the rest of my life. But the way the world was these days, and being in the service, made life so uncertain. Women were starting to fly combat missions and proving themselves as good as their male counterparts.

When Mark and I were growing up, our father was home most of the time, and even though he had stayed in the reserves, it hadn't interrupted our family time. The fact was that D.D. sometimes was gone more than our father. The world was changing for both men and women.

I was back leading the training team before the week was out. The crew seemed to be happy to have me back in the chair. It was a challenge to keep the paperwork and training records up to date. Leadership was not part of the dream I had imagined, but then, being able to fly three utterly different classes of aircraft was not either. There was a rumor that a newer version of my Prowler might be coming. I wondered if I would be around to fly it.

I was looking back on my just completed mission to the Gulf. Even today, while I was home going through the usual cleaning and clothes washing chores around my apartment, I could feel my mother's presence. For some reason, my mother was with me and guiding me all the way. I recalled one recent day in the Gulf while on a mission to take out an Iraqi radar base, my weapons officer heard me talking to someone other than him a couple of times. Once, he heard, "I've got it, mother, don't worry, I can do it."

I turned to see the weapons officer looking at me strangely and giving me one big smile and then saying, "My father still flies with me now and then." We smiled at each other. The mission was completed within a few minutes.

It was a strange feeling and yet a comforting one. D.D. had recognized it at Mark and Judy's graduation party in Pullman when my father had played the piano. Sometimes I felt that D.D. saw it before anyone else. Most women would've gotten jealous of the memory, but D.D. seemed to take it in stride.

D.D. had mentioned that she had met my mother just before she had passed away. Of course, she and her sister were impressed with Eve. But catching a man that had seemed so out of reach to D.D. was even more impressive. Life had changed through the years. But, thoughts of our mother were still in all of our minds and hearts. Mark had made the same remark. Her presence seemed to leave as soon as he was married.

The doorbell rang while I was deep in thought and I didn't realize I had tears in my eyes. Jim stood there in his flight suit with his civilian clothes on a hangar. "We are going out to dinner, aren't we?" he asked in his not so secure way, since I was still in my grubby clothes. Then he noticed that my eyes had tears in them. He hung his clothes on a doorknob, walked over, and put his arms around me.

Quietly I said, "I am getting married, and my mother will not be there."

Jim looked down at me and smiled. Privately he felt that he was not only marrying a brilliant and beautiful lady, but was marrying one who also had a heart of gold.

"Joni, remember that missile you sent that saved my ass?"

"Yes," nodding my head.

"Remember those ships your team took out in the Gulf saving a bunch of lives?"

"Yes."

"Remember when you made your first and then final aircraft landings in Texas?"

Another head nod and another "Yes."

Remember when you took out the drug boat that was trying to get away and decided to go in for the kill? And this last mission when you took out those radar towers in Iraq?"

"How did you know?"

"Well, I do know the people that fly with you. Some of them have asked about your mother. It seems whenever you are about to make an important decision, you always ask your mom to stay with you."

"Smart guy! That is the reason I am marrying you. You have all the answers!"

"Two pilots getting married to each other is a little scary, isn't it?" Then he said, "I'm sure your mother will be there when we get married, just like she always is."

Then it was dinner out at our favorite restaurant off base. Two people in love tonight, enjoying Puget Sound with the San Juan Islands spread out before us as we sat on the patio enjoying a seafood meal. We laughed and enjoyed the peaceful evening, thinking of the hectic month or two ahead. Jim could arrange his schedule so it would not interfere with our plans. I felt that I would be stateside for the next six months before shipping out again for Middle Eastern duty. "Besides," I laughed, "Who would interfere with a girl's wedding plans?"

Beginning September 15, I took a 30 day leave to help with the last minute details after D.D. had done most of the planning. Jim made one last Asian trip in the middle of the month and would be there for the final preparations. He returned home to find a registered letter from the Navy waiting for him. The letter stated that he would be recalled to duty for six months beginning October 10. It meant that the holidays together would not happen, at least not this year. "What a way to start a marriage!" he thought to himself. Since he was flying back to Montana in the morning, he decided not to tell me until we were together.

The following day he boarded the flight for Great Falls and I was there to meet him by myself. A few of the employees working the flight congratulated him on getting married. One of the flight attendants mentioned that her group wished him luck, although her group was upset that he would be off the market. With his flight bag and suitcase, he just smiled and left the flight and walked up through the jetway to his awaiting future bride. He saw her standing there with open arms, thinking she looked as sexy as ever in levies and a western shirt with the top two buttons unbuttoned. Her blonde hair falling around her shoulders made her look sexier than ever.

I informed him that I had the plane and would be flying down to Roundup to pick up his parents. His brother and sisters were already staying at a hotel in Great Falls. He then pulled me aside so we could sit down in the waiting area. Next, he pulled out the letter that he had received after returning home yesterday. I saw the return address on the envelope.

"When are you leaving?" I asked.

"October 10," he replied. All I could think about were my father and mother when he had received his letter to return to active duty. It scared me, but knowing that the world was different now gave me some comfort. We both knew this might happen, but neither of us had realized it might be so soon.

One of the airline employees caught us as we were going out the front door. "You know we give free tug rides to employees and dependents."

Jim and I looked at each other. I gave him a big smile. "I've never ridden on a tug before. Let's give it a try."

Blond hair flying and Jim trying to hold his bag, we crossed the tarmac to the private airplane parking area where one of the aviation employees waited. It would be a 37 minute flight to Roundup. Jim called his parents to let them know what time we would be arriving. I already had fueled the aircraft before meeting his incoming flight.

It was one of those Montana blue sky days. We took off from Great Falls—directing the aircraft's nose eastward towards Roundup—making our way between the Highwood Mountain Range to the north and the Little Belt Range to the south. We flew low enough to notice that the poplar trees were starting to turn to their fall colors. Jim had hunted and fished in both ranges and pointed out different landmarks along the way.

It was Jim who made the call to the Roundup airport. "Hello, young man. We are glad you have decided to visit us one more time. Congratulations on your marriage," came the voice of the airport manager. Jim thanked him and requested the local weather and permission to land. When I landed the aircraft, we could see his parents standing off the small tarmac, waiting for us to arrive. I turned the engines off and coasted most of the way to the front of the hangar. After his parents boarded the aircraft, it was maybe 15 minutes and the Cessna was racing down the runway, catching the warm fall breeze as it lifted off the ground.

Returning to the ranch in The Shadows of Sawtooth Ridge, it wasn't long before the Little Belts were left behind, and the Rockies stood tall among their counterparts. The sun was beginning to set behind them as we approached the ranch's runway. It was September and the days were starting to be shorter. It would not be long before there would be cattle feeding in the pasture just beyond the runway.

All four of us helped unload the luggage and push the aircraft into the hangar. Even with all the fuss, it seemed to be peaceful as evening approached over the ranch. In the distance, we could hear owls calling out to each other. The creek, with its gentle flow, could be heard above the silence of the early evening. I grabbed Jim by the hand and led him to the cottonwood stump by the creek. Together we sat down and listened as the evening closed in on us. We needed time together.

We could hear a trout splashing in the water, trying to catch that elusive fly. We just sat there in silence until darkness finally overtook us. Then we both got up and made our way to the house. D.D. had made sure that a warm meal still awaited us. Neither parent commented on missing the main dinner or asked any questions.

My father spent many hours on El Tocon. It had been used countless times over the years even before they were married. It was late when my father asked if we would like to see and make a run-through for the wedding. He pointed at D.D., Judy, and me with a smile. "We also have three supervisors." We all laughed as my father led the group out to the barn and the covered arena.

They had constructed a dance floor. There was a stand for the minister and the band. Chairs were sitting around the arena with tables set up in the barn for the reception afterward. I could see D.D.'s artistry all around. I said, "Thanks, mother," as I gave her one big long hug. Then I grabbed all of them in another family hug. My parents, brother and Judy had made this one beautiful event. These people were family for me. It was what I wanted and knew I would receive with Jim.

Mark stood back and looked at his wife. "We forgot to tell all of you of one more event happening in of our lives. We are expecting!" Everyone turned and gave them a surprised look. Then the smiles and the congratulations came.

The family returned to the house. Mark opened a bottle of champagne, and we shared a toast. Our father sat down to the piano and started playing an easy listening piece. D.D. sat down with one arm around the man she loved. First, he had lost a son and gained a daughter- in-law who lived nearby. Now he was losing a daughter and gaining a son-in-law who he knew and loved.

My parents were still deeply in love with each other. They managed to build a life and a family in The Shadows of Sawtooth Ridge. The world knew both of them very well. Both were still very attractive and intelligent people. Jim once said many women they worked with felt my father was the most handsome guy alive. I was still amazed that when I received my wings, there were a few of the instructors in Texas who wanted to meet my step-mother.

It was late when everyone retired to the guest cottages, leaving Jim's folks and mine in the large house. Everyone still could hear the relaxing piano music echoing over the plateau. Tomorrow would be another day, and it too would go late into the evening.

The band arrived early and started to set up their equipment. Jim spent about a half-hour with them and seemed to be deep in conversation. Just as soon as anyone walked over to join in the conversation, the discussion ended.

Meanwhile, my father played a couple of his favorite tunes an old piano which had been moved to the arena earlier in the week. It looked like it had seen better days but seemed to sound fine. The next minute Jim's father brought out his trumpet and he and D.D.'s brother-in-law started to jam together. D.D. had borrowed a guitar from one of the band members and joined in with them. I was trying to get ready for the ceremony with my maids of honor, but was having difficulty keeping my attention on the matters at hand. Cameras were clicking all over the place. Judy's parents were here, and even a couple of her brothers and sisters made it from Oregon. Many of Jim and my father's airline friends also made the trek. All morning, cars, pickups, and RVs pulled into the parking area near the venue.

A stock tank full of ice was set in a machine shed with every kind of cold drink in it. A couple of Jim's friends offered to make the meal for everyone. Mark and Judy's wedding was pretty large, but nothing like this one. Jim had managed to make theirs, but I was in the Middle East playing war, as he put it. Neither Liz nor Betsy had ever had on cowboy boots before today. However, both husbands approved the new look—boots, those tight fitting jeans and western shirts.

As the sun started to set behind the Sawtooths, the ceremony began. The band started to play Here Comes the Bride and then stopped. Everyone was looking for the bride to enter the arena when a voice that seemed to come off the Rockies started to sing Take My Hand.

Everyone in the audience almost forgot about the bride coming down the aisle. Jim's voice from heaven echoed through the air. Then a female voice from the back joined him.

Finally, it was my father and me with our hands together holding a microphone, as we made our way up to the minister and Jim, with his best man and groomsmen standing beside him. The entire group turned to face the audience after my father handed my hand to Jim and hugged me. My father whispered something into Jim's ear, and Jim smiled and said, "Yes, Sir!" The best man, groomsmen and maids of honor joined in the chorus as they finished the song.

The audience was silent as no one could figure out whether to clap or stay silent until the minister finally started clapping, and then everyone gave us a standing ovation. D.D. looked at my father and said with a smile, "She is marrying the right man." He put his arm around her and laid a gentle kiss on her forehead. The bride and groom walked down the aisle to the barn and the reception.

SUMMARY

Yes, I had found my mate, or if you hear the rest of the story, Jim had found me first. He left for the Middle East on a six month tour of duty a few weeks after the wedding. I was there to see him off. I did returned to help with the fall cattle drive without him. We also met in Singapore on his return and shared dinner again at one of our favorite restaurants.

He continued to fly for a commercial airline out of Seattle. I made a couple more tours of the Middle East and was checked out in the new upgraded E-6B before I too started to fly for an airline out of Seattle. We were both re-activated after 9/11. Both of us served our country honorably.

My father eventually retired from the airlines after commuting to Detroit and New York for a few years. Before retiring, after 9/11 he flew many more Mac trips, primarily to the Middle East. He retired to the ranch in The Shadows of Sawtooth Ridge.

Dakota is still writing, and someday we will hear the rest of her story.

www.ingramcontent.com/pod-product-compliance
Lightning Source LLC
LaVergne TN
LVHW011934070526
838202LV00054B/4645